# "You're so beautiful," he said hoarsely...

He gave a moan and brought his mouth down on hers in a long kiss, but this time his lips were gentle, not angry, caressing, lulling her. A sense of delicious languor filled her and her breath quickened. Forgetting all caution, she abandoned herself, throwing her arms around him, pulling him to her.

"Pippa, I want you so...I want you so badly...."

The repetition of this phrase brought Phillippa from the brink of surrender. That he wanted her, she had no doubt, but he did not love her, and without his love she could not give herself to him.

Using every last ounce of willpower left she put both hands against his chest and pushed him away.

"No! Damon...no. Please...I...I can't! Please stop!"

# WELCOME
# TO THE WONDERFUL WORLD
# OF *Harlequin Romances*

Interesting, informative and entertaining,
each Harlequin Romance portrays an appealing
and original love story. With a varied array
of settings, we may lure you on an African safari,
to a quaint Welsh village, or an exotic Riviera
location—anywhere and everywhere that adventurous
men and women fall in love.

As publishers of Harlequin Romances, we're
extremely proud of our books. Since 1949,
Harlequin Enterprises has built its publishing
reputation on the solid base of quality and
originality. Our stories are the most popular
paperback romances sold in North America; every
month, six new titles are released and sold at
nearly every book-selling store in Canada and the
United States.

A free catalog listing all Harlequin Romances
can be yours by writing to the

HARLEQUIN READER SERVICE,
(In the U.S.) 1440 South Priest Drive, Tempe, AZ 85281
(In Canada) Stratford, Ontario, N5A 6W2

We sincerely hope you enjoy reading
this Harlequin Romance.

Yours truly,

THE PUBLISHERS
*Harlequin Romances*

# Seeds of April

## Celia Scott

# Harlequin Books

TORONTO • NEW YORK • LONDON
AMSTERDAM • PARIS • SYDNEY • HAMBURG
STOCKHOLM • ATHENS • TOKYO • MILAN

Original hardcover edition published in 1983
by Mills & Boon Limited

ISBN 0-373-02568-8

Harlequin Romance first edition August 1983

You'll love me yet!—and I can tarry
Your love's protracted growing;
June reared that bunch of flowers you carry,
From seeds of April's sowing.

Robert Browning, *Pippa Passes*

# CHAPTER ONE

WITH infinite care Philippa Kenmore filled the fragile interior of the gâteau Saint-Honoré with rich cream. Laying the empty pastry-bag aside, she absently tucked a wandering strand of honey-beige hair behind her ear and gave a sigh of satisfaction. Without a doubt this gâteau was the best she'd ever baked. She consulted her loose-leaf business diary to check the rest of the menu Damon Everett had ordered for this evening's dinner party.

'Caviare'—that was easy, he always had jars and jars of it in his fridge, and he'd phoned earlier to tell her he had bought porterhouse steaks. All she had to do was pick up some fresh vegetables on her way to Wimbledon, and leave herself enough time to prepare a soup, in case his guest didn't like caviare. The next notation read—'Salad'—a simple one, with a tang of lemon. 'Rich dessert'—well, the Saint-Honoré was rich all right. If he doesn't like it, Philippa thought, there's no pleasing the man. Not that Damon Everett found fault with her catering, it seemed. He had been hiring her to cook for him regularly for two months now. And apart from the fact that he didn't seem to like her any more than she did him, he never voiced any complaints. Indeed, he often paid her compliments about her culinary skills. But his compliments were delivered with a hint of mockery that made her wary of him.

She checked the time and realised she was running later than she thought. Dashing into the bedroom of the ground floor flat she shared with her younger sister Martha, she hastily changed out of blue jeans and

pulled on one of her 'working uniforms', a plain
brown skirt and cream blouse with a tan belt buckled
around her slim waist.

She tugged her glossy hair back and fastened it with
an elastic band, peering into the mirror that hung
above an old desk Martha used as a dressing table. She
had to stoop to do this, because she was a very tall girl.
Philippa stood five foot ten inches in her stockinged
feet, and being slender as a reed she appeared taller.
All her life she had towered over her peers, including
her diminutive sister. Very subtly Martha had
managed to instil into her older sister the notion that
Philippa was a freak, clumsy, oversized, and graceless.
And over the years Philippa had started to believe this
propaganda. She felt like Gulliver among the
Lilliputians. When she looked in the mirror she saw
her reflection with Martha's eyes. She didn't see a
good-looking young woman of twenty-seven with
glorious ash-blonde hair that fell in waves below her
shoulders. She didn't see the extraordinary hazel eyes,
fringed with thick lashes that were naturally dark, and
didn't need the liberal coats of mascara that Martha
had to apply—eyes that seemed amber in some lights,
golden in others. The fact that her skin was flawless,
her figure slender, and her legs long and shapely,
seemed to escape her scrutiny. And she seemed to do
her level best to spoil the beauty nature had given her.
She wore nothing but 'sensible' skirts and blouses,
always chose the flattest shoes she could find, and
scraped her shining mane back into a punishing
elastic-banded ponytail.

She left the glamour to Martha, since she was
always far too busy with her catering business, and far
too tired, to have time for herself. It had been that way
for some years now. The girls' father had been killed
in a car crash when they were small. Mrs Kenmore
was a tiny, helpless scrap of a woman who had been

protected all her life. In her widowhood she turned to her capable eldest daughter for help, and spoiled her baby, Martha, rotten. After school Philippa organised the household, cooked, and did any odd jobs going. And she did it cheerfully, since her nature, like her father's had been, was practical and good-natured.

Mrs Kenmore had died when Philippa was eighteen, and the loss of her doting mother caused Martha to suffer a breakdown. Philippa had somehow managed to cope with her own grief, her distraught sister, and work towards her diploma at the Cordon Bleu Cookery School she attended. By the time Martha recovered she was totally dependent on her elder sister, and Philippa found it difficult to teach her to be less demanding. The damage Mrs Kenmore had started with her indulgence was completed by Martha's illness, and Philippa was trapped. She thought of moving away to live on her own, but knowing what a scene Martha would create, she had put it off.

There were other disadvantages to living with Martha. Since she was wickedly extravagant by nature, her share of the rent often went on clothes she 'simply couldn't resist', and Philippa had to wait months before being paid back. When she reminded her sister that she needed the cash she was sharply told—'Don't be a money-grubber, Tusker, it's boring!' The nickname 'Tusker' had been coined many years ago by their mother because she had considered her eldest daughter to be the 'elephant of the family'. Philippa had protested, but her wishes had been ignored, and she'd learnt to live with it.

Pulling on her penny loafers, she heard the front door slam, and suddenly Martha burst into the bedroom. Flinging her coat on to the bed and kicking her shoes to opposite sides of the room, she said,

'You still here, Tusker? Don't you have to work

tonight?' She started to undress, which in Martha's case meant pulling off her clothes and letting them fall to the floor.

Philippa checked her watch. 'It's only three-thirty, Martha,' she said. 'What are you doing home at this hour?'

'They let me come home because I told them I wasn't feeling well,' her sister replied, grabbing her hairbrush and attacking her short curly hair vigorously. Her hair was darker blonde than Philippa's and lacked the luminous beige quality of her sister's.

'What's wrong, honey?' Philippa asked, concerned.

'Nothing. I told them I didn't feel well because this divine man's picking me up at five and . . .'

'Man? What man?'

'This dreamy man I met at work today. Don't just stand there, Tusker!' Martha snapped. 'I've only got an hour and a half and I must have a bath. Iron my pink silk dress, will you? The new one.'

'Now just hold it a moment, Martha!' Philippa cut in. 'Do you mean to tell me you pretended to be ill just to go on a date with a man you've only just met?'

Exasperated, Martha flung down her brush and headed for the bathroom, followed by Philippa. Irritably she turned on the tap and started to fill the ancient tub. Her childish face was petulant.

'Don't nag, Tusker,' she said crossly, 'you're such a bore when you nag.'

'I don't mean to nag you Martha, but I'm worried you'll lose *this* job too. You're always pretending to be ill. Remember, you waited a long time for this job.'

Indeed, Martha had been fired from her previous job for absenteeism, and had spent several months, not searching for work particularly hard, taking an extended holiday. She had never offered to pay Philippa back rent for these months, and flew into a fury whenever the subject was broached.

'Oh, don't fuss, for God's sake!' she said venomously. 'You're like an old woman sometimes—fuss,
fuss, fuss!' With an ugly pout she threw a handful of
bathsalts into the steaming water, and the sweet odour
of violets filled the small bathroom. Philippa decided
to try another tack.

'Who is this man you're going out with?'

'His name's Eric. He came into the travel agency
today. He's dreamy!'

'So you mentioned. What about Ray?' Ray was
Martha's current boy-friend.

'That creep!' Martha's lip curled with disgust.

'That's not what you said about him last week. You
said he was the greatest.'

'I hadn't met Eric then.'

'I see. And what has this Eric got that Ray hasn't?'

'A car, for one thing,' her sister answered blithely,
'and he's much better looking.'

'What about Ray? Does he know he's been replaced
in your affections?'

'Not yet. I told him I wasn't feeling well enough to
go out tonight. I'll tell him to get lost tomorrow,' she
added with a giggle.

'Do you mean to say you had a date with Ray
tonight and you ditched him for a stranger! Honestly,
Martha! That's an unforgivable way to behave!'

'Now, Tusker, don't scold, there's a dear,' said
Martha, turning on the charm. 'Ray was becoming a
dreadful nuisance—begging me to go away with him
for weekends. A real pain!' Frankly Philippa didn't
think that would bother Martha in the slightest, but
she held her peace.

'I still don't think Ray's pestering gives you the
right to skip work, Martha.'

'Oh, shut up, Tusker!' Martha's tone was vitriolic.
'Just because you're not attractive to men, there's no
need to take it out on me!'

'That's a nasty thing to say!' retorted Philippa, defending herself from this attack.

'Nasty or not, it's true.' Martha turned off the bathwater. 'Let's face it, Phil, you're too tall, too old, and no fun. Men don't like women like you.'

Philippa felt the colour drain from her face. Her height was her Achilles heel. Martha knew that and used it ruthlessly. True, Philippa didn't have her younger sister's track record with boy-friends, but there had been men in her life, and if these relationships had not developed it had not been because of a lack in Philippa. She possessed a fastidiousness her sister did not share. And a blazing honesty, which sometimes intimidated her men friends.

She recovered herself. 'I'm afraid I can't continue this fascinating discussion about my sexual attractiveness right now, because I have to go to work.' She checked her watch again and gave a howl of panic. 'Lord, I'm late!' She headed for the kitchen, and the delicate task of fitting the gâteau Saint-Honoré into a cake-box. Martha's wail followed her.

'But, Tusker, my dress! It needs ironing!'

'You know where the iron is, Martha. See you later.' Philippa grabbed her raincoat and balancing the precious cake-box like a dozen loose eggs went to her old Mini that was parked outside.

After picking up the fresh vegetables she drove to Damon Everett's house. It was a fair distance from Hammersmith to Wimbledon, so she had time to think. Not that her thoughts were too pleasant. What to do about Martha? Ideally they should find separate flats, but that was easier said than done. After Martha's long stint of unemployment Philippa's savings were low, and the flats she could afford, within reasonable distance of her clients, were as rare as hen's teeth. A frown creased her smooth brow as she drove through the dappled spring sunshine on her way to work for Damon Everett.

She vividly remembered her meeting with him two months ago. She had been cooking for one of her regulars, a Mrs Cardew. 'Divinity Fudge on Chocolate Leaves' was the note against Mrs Cardew's name in Philippa's business diary. This way she kept a record of her clients' favourite dishes, and she tended to think of her regulars by their favourite foods rather than their names. So Mrs Cardew was 'Divinity' to her cook.

It had been a small party, just four people, she remembered. But one of the four was an arresting-looking man who dominated the room. He must have been close to six foot four, and was blessed with broad shoulders and a strong muscular frame, that tapered to lean hips and long legs. His face was dark-complexioned and austerely handsome, with stern lines running from his jutting nose to his particularly well defined mouth. His dark brown hair was cut fashionably trim. He was dressed meticulously, and carried himself with an air.

That particular night in Divinity's kitchen, when dinner was over, Philippa was scraping and stacking dishes (she always left the washing-up for the client to deal with) when suddenly Mrs Cardew came in accompanied by the enormous man Philippa had noticed in the dining room. He had loomed in the doorway, dwarfing his hostess.

'Damon, this is my treasure,' Divinity had twittered, 'Miss Kenmore, I'd like you to meet Mr Damon Everett . . . the Damon Everett. He thought your dinner an absolute *dream*, and I said he should tell you so himself.'

Philippa wasn't at all sure who *the* Damon Everett was, but it was apparent she was supposed to. The name was vaguely familiar, but she couldn't place it, and she felt annoyed with Mrs Cardew, who was more than a trifle silly, for introducing him that way. It fed the man's vanity, a trait she felt sure someone so unusual-looking possessed. His uncompromising steel-blue eyes regarded Philippa unwaveringly. She had resented this scrutiny, and had half turned away from him to continue her work.

'Congratulations on an excellent dinner, Miss Kenmore,' he said. His voice was very distinctive, deep and resonant.

'We aim to please.' She stacked the dishes with maximum clatter.

'I've given Mr Everett your phone number, Miss Kenmore,' Divinity gushed, 'he's *so* impressed with your cooking. He wants to hire you for a dinner party at his home. What do you think of *that*?' She twinkled roguishly at Philippa, who slapped another pan into the sink. 'Mr Everett's very fussy,' Divinity reproved. 'Well, he would be, wouldn't he? Financing and running tiptop hotels all over the world.' She beamed at her guests, who looked rather discomfited.

Now the penny dropped! Philippa remembered reading an article about him. 'The resourceful Damon Everett, Hotel Empire-Builder,' had been the caption.

'I'm overcome,' she said, 'but I'm also overbooked.' She turned to face him, tilting her head, in spite of her five feet ten inches, to look him full in the eyes. 'Perhaps one of the employees at one of your tiptop hotels could cook for you.'

'I want you to cook for me,' he replied quietly. 'I'm planning a dinner party in ten days' time at my home in Wimbledon. For seven people. I don't want a complicated menu.'

Here was a man who was used to getting his own way. Philippa opened her mouth to protest this high-handed treatment, but he forestalled her by handing her his business card.

'Phone me with your decision. Goodnight, Miss Kenmore.' He held the door for Mrs Cardew, and they swept out.

And that had been that. She decided she disliked the overbearing Damon Everett, but contrary to what she had told him she was quite free the night he planned his party. And, since she needed the money, she phoned to accept the job. She reasoned that he was a good contact, and she mustn't let her personal dislike get in the way of business.

The dinner given at his luxurious Wimbledon house was a great success. Damon Everett was named 'Beef Wellington Rare' and referred to as 'Wellington' ever afterwards in the diary. Soon she was driving her Mini to cook in his huge modern kitchen about twice a week.

She turned into the gravelled drive and parked at the back of the house. Her little car looked quite shabby compared to the shining silver-grey Jaguar that stood in the garage. That meant he was already home. She wouldn't have to look for the key in its usual hiding place.

Balancing her precious cake, she went into the lofty kitchen. The house was an old one, sitting right on Wimbledon Common, so that it had an air of being a country home in spite of being in the heart of London. It had been restored without being spoilt. The kitchen had been completely done over, and Philippa considered it a dream, with its double refrigerator, and every appliance she could wish for. She was inspired to dazzling heights of culinary inventiveness, and black truffles encased in fragile feather-light pastry, duck stuffed with pine nuts and brought to the table flambéed in brandy, and once a baked Alaska, her first and a triumph, made their way to the candlelit dining room. Tonight's dinner was going to be a snap compared to some of her previous ones.

She had just tied her apron and was scrubbing new potatoes—the size of her thumbnail—when Damon Everett came into the kitchen. He was still wearing a grey pin-stripe business suit and was carrying a large cardboard box, which clinked when he put it on the table. He nodded briefly and proceeded to unload the box, which turned out to contain bottles of champagne. His large, well-shaped hands deftly lifted the green-black bottles and stood them gently on the long refectory table, then he put them in the fridge.

'There!' he said, smiling at Philippa. 'That should hold us for a bit.'

'Are you planning a party?' she asked, tipping the tiny potatoes into a pan and starting to clean asparagus for soup.

'No. But I like to have plenty of champagne on ice for emergencies.'

'Emergencies?' Startled, she turned and looked into his mocking blue eyes.

'Well—pleasant emergencies. Like someone getting married. And I like to drink it myself. Don't you?'

'I've only ever drunk it at weddings.'

'And did you enjoy it, Miss Kenmore?' He raised an eyebrow and looked down into her face, and she flushed, as she always did under that ironic gaze. Placing the delicate green asparagus into a tall pot, she answered him crisply.

'Yes, I enjoyed it. But I've never drunk it by the *gallon*!' This sounded so rude that she turned bright red and stammered. 'W-what I mean is, I've never seen so much champagne at one time. Except at weddings, of course——!' she trailed off, feeling foolish.

'Would you like a glass? There is some chilled.'

'What? *Now*?' She was taken aback.

'Don't look so scandalised, Miss Kenmore,' he said, 'I'm not offering you a whole bottle. Just a friendly glass of champagne while you prepare dinner.'

'Well . . . yes. Thank you.' She turned her attention to making a roux for the soup, casting a sidelong look at her employer from under her long lashes. What had got into him? He didn't usually behave like this. If it was possible she could have sworn he was nervous.

'Here you are.' He handed her a long narrow glass of wine. 'I'll have one as well, I think.' He poured a second glass and raised it in a toast. 'Here's to . . . to the dinner. Which I'm sure will be delicious as always.'

Philippa took a sip of champagne, which tickled her nose delightfully. 'About dinner, Mr Everett,' she said, trying to restore a businesslike atmosphere, 'you said you wanted caviare to begin, but I'm making some cream of asparagus soup, just in case. And do you want the steak served on toast with pâté? I see there's pâté in the fridge.'

Damon Everett looked discomfited, and looked down to examine the champagne that bubbled in his glass. 'About my guest——' he began.

'Incidentally,' Philippa cut in, 'you did specify a rich sweet, so I made a gâteau Saint-Honoré. It's rather a lot for two, but you can finish it later in the week. It'll keep in the fridge.'

'I'd better change,' he said suddenly, putting his glass of champagne on the table and bolting out of the kitchen.

This most uncharacteristic behaviour puzzled Philippa. He seemed under some kind of emotional strain. But it had nothing to do with her, she reasoned, so she went back to making her soup.

She set the dining room table. She knew where things were kept now, and could manage this without a search for utensils. She laid two places close together at the polished oak table. As usual she took pleasure in handling the heavy Georgian silver that Damon Everett possessed. A fire was burning in the large fireplace, which set off the chill of the April evening. The flames vied with the setting sun, which glowed on the oak panelling and turned the shallow silver bowl of yellow crocuses in the centre of the table to dazzling gold. This room, like the kitchen, was spotless. Philippa wondered how many cleaning women he employed to keep the house so sparkling. She had never seen a servant about the place.

The soup was simmering, the salad waiting to be tossed, the toast ready to be spread with pâté. Once his guest arrived she could boil the potatoes and dinner would be under way. She was sipping her wine, enjoying the festive feeling champagne always gave her, when Damon Everett returned. He was now wearing a wine velvet smoking jacket. The deep red colour gave his dark-skinned face an exotic look, and made his eyes seem brighter.

He went to the glass of champagne he had left on the kitchen table and emptied it down the sink.

'Flat,' he explained, when she looked askance. 'Anyway, I don't want any more champagne. I thought a red Burgundy to go with the steaks. I've got a bottle of Chambertin open to breathe. Will Chambertin do?'

Wine was not in Philippa's province. She took care of the food, and left the wine to the client.

'I'm sure it'll be fine, Mr Everett.' She couldn't make out what was the matter with him this evening. 'Does your guest like Chambertin?'

'I don't know. I don't know what wine she likes.'

So his guest was a woman. She must be quite a special date to make him so nervous. He was most unlike his usual urbane self. He's positively human, Philippa thought; it's nice to know the imperturbable Damon Everett has nerves like the rest of us.

'Well, Miss Kenmore,' he took a deep breath and fixed his eyes on hers, 'I think it's time to serve the caviare.'

'But, Mr Everett, your guest hasn't arrived yet.'

'She has.'

'I didn't hear the bell.'

'Miss Kenmore, you're my guest this evening.' He stared fixedly into her astonished face.

'I beg your pardon?'

'No one else is coming. So I hope you'll have dinner with me.'

Philippa stared up at him.

'But, Mr Everett, if your party has fallen through you should have called me to cancel. I would have understood.'

'Well, I didn't call,' he barked at her, 'so *will* you dine with me? I want to discuss a ... a project ... with you.'

'We don't have to have dinner to discuss business,' Philippa protested. 'You could have phoned me.'

'I'm offering you a meal, Miss Kenmore. Whether you join me or not I'd appreciate it if you'd start serving,' he said, resuming his imperious manner. 'I'm very hungry.'

Without another word Philippa switched on the electric ring under the potatoes. 'I'll give you your caviare now, *sir*,' she said icily.

'And you'll join me? Come, Miss Kenmore, I'm not accustomed to begging.' When she didn't reply he added, 'Pax, Miss Kenmore?' His stern face looking suddenly like a small boy's.

She fiddled with the dish of hardboiled eggs that accompanied the first course. 'Very well, Mr Everett,' she finally agreed. 'But I don't want to be paid for tonight's work.'

'If you insist.'

'I do.' She raised her delicately moulded chin defiantly.

'Now that's settled can we please eat? I missed lunch today.'

It felt odd to be sitting at the long dining table. Philippa had removed her apron while Damon lit the white candles in the branched silver candelabrum, and now she sat beside him eating caviare.

'You haven't given yourself much,' he remarked.

'It's plenty, thank you,' she answered primly, then confessed, 'I don't like it very much.'

'You don't like caviare?' He seemed amazed.

'It reminds me of salty sago pudding, and I hate sago pudding.'

'What a confession for a Cordon Bleu!' he said loftily.

'Oh, I have very plebian tastes, Mr Everett. My favourite meal is egg and chips, followed by treacle pudding.' Airily she left to get the soup. Supercilious prig! Let him digest *that*, she thought.

The remainder of the meal passed without incident. The thick steaks were juicy and tender, and the accompanying mushrooms perfect, and she'd been right about the lemon dressing on the salad. As for the gâteau Saint-Honoré, it was frankly superb. Philippa unashamedly had two helpings. She hardly touched her wine, though, even though it slid into her mouth like velvet. She wanted her wits about her this evening.

She served coffee, which they drank still seated at the table. It was dark outside the windows now, and Damon drew the red velvet curtains and threw another log on the fire. He always had coffee served in large cups of dark blue china rimmed with gold. A demitasse would look like a thimble in his big hand. He offered her a liqueur, which she refused, and after pouring himself a brandy, said,

'I'm going away soon, Miss Kenmore, and I'll be gone for quite some time.'

'I'll miss catering for you, Mr Everett. Perhaps you'll mention my name to some of your friends ...'

He ignored her interruption and went on. 'I've been watching you these past weeks, and I've decided you're an extremely capable young woman.'

'Thank you.'

'Don't interrupt.' Philippa bit her lip with annoyance and poured more coffee.

'As I said, I've been watching you, and I've decided to approach you regarding a ... a venture ... I'm about to embark on.'

She waited, but he didn't continue, so she ventured an encouraging, 'Yes?'

'I'm going to open a chain of hotels in Crete this summer,' he went on. 'I intend to supervise the operation ...'

'How interesting.'

'Please be quiet!' He didn't raise his voice, but this was said with such intensity that she was stunned to silence. 'I'm leaving for Crete in approximately two weeks, but there's one small hitch.'

'Indeed?' What on earth has this to do with me? she wondered.

'Yes. Now, Crete is rather an old-fashioned island, and I have a fourteen-year-old niece, my ward Athena. She's away at school, but she's joining me in Crete for the summer. My associates feel, and I agree with them, that while I'm in Crete with a fourteen-year-old girl in my care, it would be preferable if I ... if I were married.' Again he fell silent, his blue eyes never left her face.

'I understand,' Philippa said helpfully.

'I wonder if you do,' he said. 'I intend to get myself a wife.'

'And you want me to cater for the wedding breakfast?' Philippa cut in. 'Well, it would depend on the number of guests, and the amount of time ...'

'*Shut up, Philippa!*' It was the first time he had called her by her first name, and he sounded so ferocious she was quite scared.

'I'm asking you to come to Crete as my wife.' Her large amber-tinted eyes grew enormous. 'It would be strictly a business arrangement, of course. I would ask you to help with the entertaining that I'll be doing . . .'

'Y-you mean cook for you?' she gasped.

'Don't be idiotic,' his tone was cutting, 'I have staff for that. No, I want you for my hostess, and to keep an eye on Athena, be a companion to the girl.'

'Bu-but why me?' Philippa still found it hard to grasp that he'd asked her to *marry* him.

'I've told you, you strike me as an eminently capable young woman. The job requires someone down-to-earth.'

'You think of marriage as a *job*?'

'In this case it would be a job, a business agreement. And you'd be getting a bargain, I think.'

'A bargain? To be married to you?' His conceit was monumental!

He fixed her with his laser-beam glare. 'Try not to be deliberately stupid, Philippa. The bargain would be the trip to Crete, a lot of free time, plus a new wardrobe. I'll supply suitable clothes of course. I call that a bargain, don't you?'

She ignored this and said, 'You say you want a companion for your niece?'

'For Athena, yes.'

'Then why not hire one? I don't see why you have to go to the extreme of getting married.'

For some unaccountable reason colour slowly flooded his face and his usually steady eyes wavered. 'I told you, Crete is a very . . . er . . . conservative place. It would be . . . be difficult, to say the least.' He tilted his glass and examined his brandy intently. 'There would be gossip . . . talk.'

'I find that hard to believe, Mr Everett.' She willed him to look at her. 'Even in a place like Crete.'

'Nevertheless——' Again his eyes left hers. 'And there's another reason . . .' She waited patiently for him to continue.

'Yes?'

'Athena is an orphan. She needs . . . she needs stability. A hired companion wouldn't be good for her; she had that last year. She needs to feel . . . that she's part of a family.'

'A *fake* family! That won't be good for her, surely?'

'I know my niece better than you,' he sounded shifty. 'Besides, there's still the question of propriety. I tell you it's essential I have a legal wife while I'm working in Crete.' He looked at her obliquely. 'I've thought this out very carefully, I assure you.'

'What about later on?' Philippa countered. 'When the Greek job is finished and you . . . we . . . return to England? What then?'

'An amicable divorce.'

'Very stable for your niece,' she observed drily.

'Athena will adjust. She's a very resilient child. And by then, I hope the two of you will be friends. She can continue seeing you from time to time if you both wish. She doesn't have to be hurt.'

'Divorce hurts everyone,' said Philippa, her mouth grim.

'Not our sort of divorce,' he replied loftily. 'Ours will be a business arrangement. My lawyer will draw up a contract for you to sign. I'll naturally reimburse you for any loss of income during your stay in Crete. I'm assuming, of course, that you're not already attached to some young man?'

'I'm quite free.'

'I thought as much,' he said smugly. He thinks I'm too dull to have a man in my life, I suppose, Philippa thought sourly, looking daggers at him.

'I think you're absolutely mad!' she said. 'We don't even like each other.' In the quiet that followed she could hear the ash falling from the logs in the fireplace.

'But that's precisely why I thought of you,' he answered finally. 'The last thing I want is an emotional entanglement. This way it's strictly business and no one gets hurt.' He took a sip of brandy, the enormous balloon glass looking fragile in his strong hand. 'Don't make your mind up right away. Phone me in a couple of days with your decision.'

He helped her clear the cups into the kitchen. He insisted she take the remainder of the gâteau Saint-Honoré with her, bundled her out to her car, and watched her drive away, his tall figure silhouetted against the bright kitchen doorway.

Philippa drove home through the dark, her headlights sweeping across the tangle of trees that grew along the edge of the common. Bitterly she went over the events of the evening. Trust Damon Everett to make even a proposal of marriage sound insulting! No woman enjoys being told that she could never become an emotional entanglement, not even when it is the last thing she wants herself. He annoyed her so—being charming one minute, and rude the next. She never knew where she stood with the wretched man. In her irritation she pressed down on the accelerator and drove home over the speed limit.

When she opened the door of the flat a smell of burning greeted her. The ironing board was still standing in the living room with a red-hot iron scorching a hole in it. Grim-lipped, she unplugged it, and using an oven mitt, carried the iron into the kitchen. The board was ruined. Martha had obviously ironed her dress.

Shaking with anger and fear—fire was a terror of Philippa's—she got ready for bed, but was far too tense to sleep, so she tried to concentrate on a novel until she had calmed down. She heard Martha's key in

the lock long after midnight, and that young lady
bounced into the bedroom and started stepping out of
her pink dress, leaving it in a heap on the floor.

'Hi, Tusker. What's the funny smell?'

'The funny smell is the smell of burning, Martha. I
assume you ironed your dress before you left tonight.'
Martha's dark brown eyes went blank with guilt.

'So?'

'So you left the iron on. It's lucky I came in when I
did. You could have burnt the place down.' Philippa
waited for an apology, but Martha's face became
cantankerous.

'If you'd ironed my dress for me, Tusker, it
wouldn't have happened!'

'Are you seriously suggesting it's *my* fault that you
nearly burnt us to a crisp?' Philippa asked coldly.

'No. But Eric arrived and I was in such a rush I
forgot. Anyone can forget, Tusker. Don't nag!'

'I bloody well will nag!' Philippa exploded with an
uncharactistic display of temper. 'Particularly when
it's something as serious as fire. You *must* learn to be
more careful. It's not the first time this has happened.'

'Oh, all *right*! You've made your point, now shut
up!' Martha flounced into the bathroom and started to
remove her make-up.

With a sigh Philippa put aside her book. This had
been a trying day. She was tired, and she had plenty to
occupy her thoughts without having to cope with
another of her sister's moods.

Martha, wielding her toothbrush, poked her head
through the doorway to say, 'Are you committed to
any heavy-duty dinners this weekend, Tusker?'

Philippa was instantly alert. This kind of question
from Martha usually meant a heavy-duty favour.

'Why?'

'Because I forgot to mention that I've invited some
people over for dinner on Saturday.'

'How many people?'

'About twelve.'

'*Twelve*?' Philippa shot bolt upright in her bed.

'Well ... fourteen, actually,' said Martha, 'and I invited Eric too. Is it a problem?'

'A *problem*? Are you out of your mind? Saturday's the day after tomorrow ...'

'Which gives you tomorrow to shop,' Martha said complacently. 'I promised them *spaghetti pescatora* made from your own pasta.'

Philippa's tawny eyes grew frantic. She pushed a slim hand through her silky blonde hair and started to twist it in her agitation.

'Why didn't you tell me earlier, Martha? I'm catering a cocktail party tomorrow, and I won't have time. Good *pescatora* takes forever to prepare, you know that!'

'Well, you could make an early start on Saturday. I invited everybody for seven, so it should give you time. You could make an easy dessert.'

'Easy dessert!' Philippa exploded, 'I could wring your neck! I'll need help. Keep Saturday free—you can do the shopping.'

'But, Tusker, I promised to play tennis with Eric if the weather's nice!'

'Pray for rain,' her sister answered grimly.

'Don't be difficult,' Martha whined. 'You're not doing anything on Saturday, I'll bet. Knowing you, you were probably going to spend your time reading some boring old cookbook.'

'I'd hoped to get a bit of rest this weekend, as a matter of fact.' Philippa looked at the bedside clock. 'Catch up on my sleep.'

'Well, have an early night after you've cooked the dinner.'

Philippa raised a surprised eyebrow. 'Do our guests plan to leave early, then?'

'Er . . . no . . . but you won't be missed if you go to bed.'

'Thanks very much, Martha,' snapped Philippa, hurt. Martha returned to the bathroom to finish brushing her teeth, talking through the process.

'Don't look so cross, Tusker. I mean, let's face it, they're my friends, not yours.'

'I'm needed to prepare the feast, but not to attend, is that it?'

Martha rinsed her mouth noisily and came back into the bedroom. 'Let's face it, Phil, you won't be missed.' She noticed Philippa's face and went on testily, 'Tusker, be realistic! My friends are . . . well . . . *trendy*. You don't have anything in common with them.' She turned her back on Philippa and settled herself for sleep.

Without planning it Philippa heard herself say, 'Your trendy friends will have to make do with cold ham and salad, Martha. I won't have time to prepare anything more elaborate. I plan to spend most of Saturday shopping for my trousseau.'

Nothing happened for a moment, then Martha turned round to face her sister, her brown eyes hard as pebbles.

'Impossible!' she said finally.

'Why impossible?'

'Well, you never go out with anyone.'

'I don't tell you everything I do.'

Martha's face was a mask of suspicion. 'Who are you marrying?'

'His name is Damon—Damon Everett.'

'You don't mean the Damon Everett who's in all the papers?' Martha squealed.

'Yes. Mr Everett . . . er . . . Damon has been getting a lot of publicity just lately,' Philippa agreed.

'How on earth did you meet him?'

'Through my job.'

'When?'

'Two months ago.'

'Why didn't you tell me *then*?' There was an aggrieved note in Martha's voice.

'He only asked me tonight,' Philippa admitted.

Martha continued her relentless inquisition. 'When do you plan to get married?'

'It's not quite certain. In about two weeks.'

'*Two weeks!* Why so soon? Tusker, you're not . . .?'

'Of course not. Don't be silly, Martha,' Philippa cut in hastily. 'It's because Mr . . . er . . . Damon has to go to Crete . . . to work. He wants us to be married first, so it will be a . . . a sort of honeymoon,' she finished lamely.

'But what about me?' Martha wailed. 'What am I supposed to do?'

'You'll be all right, Martha. I'll pay my share of the rent until you find another girl to share.'

'I don't want to share with anyone else.'

'Well, until you find a smaller place, then.'

'I don't want to live alone.' Martha's lower lip trembled.

'From the number of young men who come hammering on our door asking for you I think you'll be getting married yourself pretty soon.'

'That's different,' Martha said illogically. 'I thought you were happy here with me,' she whined. 'Why do you have to change things? Why do you have to get married?'

Philippa looked into her sister's discontented face. 'Has it never crossed your mind that I have the right to a life of my own, Martha?' When she didn't reply Philippa persisted, 'Hasn't it occurred to you that I might fall madly in love one day?'

Martha's expression grew ugly. 'Don't make me *laugh*, Tusker!'

'Well, I *am* madly in love. And furthermore . . .'

Philippa leaned on her elbow and faced her sister, '*furthermore*, Damon feels the same way. He doesn't want to wait a moment longer than necessary.' Martha started to protest, but Philippa cut her short. 'I won't hear another word. Let's both go to sleep. It's late, and tomorrow's a working day.'

She snapped off the light and turned her back, but the younger girl wasn't going to give in so easily. She argued and complained, and only when the sky showed the first streaks of dawn did she fall into an exhausted sleep.

Philippa lay beside her sleeping sister rigid with panic. She was committed to marrying Damon Everett now, for if she refused his offer Martha would assume she had succeeded in getting her own way yet again, and Philippa would be even more trapped. She reasoned that her 'marriage' would only be for a couple of months, long enough to teach Martha a much-needed lesson. She only hoped the lesson wouldn't rebound on her. Remembering her lie to Martha that she and Damon were 'madly in love', she was filled with dread. She sensed that Damon was a man to be reckoned with, and she hoped she could keep her side of the bargain without upsetting him. She suspected that her future husband kept a tight rein on a fiery temper, and she didn't fancy provoking him into losing it.

## CHAPTER TWO

PHILIPPA waited until she had finally got Martha off to work next morning before phoning Damon. Martha had been fretful and overtired, and would have stayed away from the travel agency if Philippa hadn't pointed out that her record of absenteeism was pretty high, and she couldn't afford to get fired now. This had brought on fresh recriminations about Philippa's coming marriage and desertion. Finally she had left, and Philippa picked up the phone with a trembling hand. Her heart threatened to burst out of the neat navy blue flannel dressing-gown she was wearing, it was beating so hard.

The phone was answered by Damon's secretary, a businesslike female, who asked Philippa to repeat her name, since she was inaudible with nervousness. While Philippa hung on waiting for him to come on the line, she had to control herself not to hang up.

'Everett speaking.' He *did* have the most beautiful voice, its rich timbre sent a shiver down her spine.

'Good morning, Mr Everett. It's Philippa Kenmore.' She was annoyed that her own voice sounded like Kermit the frog's, her throat was so dry.

'Philippa. Yes?' He wasn't making it any easier for her.

'About your ... er ... proposal ...'

'Yes?' She cursed him silently; couldn't the wretched man say anything else!

'I've been thinking it over ... and ...' she trailed off, but he didn't say a word, 'and I've decided to accept,' she finished in a rush. There was silence the other end of the line. 'Did you hear me, Mr Everett?'

For a dreadful moment she wondered if he had changed his mind. Then he spoke. His voice sounded perfectly ordinary, which irritated her.

'Good. Can you meet me this evening to go into the arrangements?' He sounded as cool as if he was discussing the menu for one of his dinner parties.

'No, I can't. I'm working this evening,' she answered shortly.

'How about lunch?'

'As long as it's early. I have to shop for a cocktail party I'm doing tonight.'

'Let's meet in Knightsbridge, then, it's midway between my office and your home.' He named an exclusive Knightsbridge restaurant. 'Will twelve-thirty suit you?'

'Perfectly,' she said crisply, and hung up. She was shaking with fury. His offhand manner was insulting. If she'd told him she was preparing grapefruit instead of soup for one of her dinners, he couldn't have sounded more uninterested. She spent the remainder of the morning baking cheese straws, light as cobwebs, for her party that night, and fighting the urge to ring him back and cancel the whole deal.

The restaurant was a cavern of hushed elegance. Philippa told herself that the head waiter . . . who was considerably shorter than she . . . did not look up at her disdainfully, but secretly she felt that he did, and this succeeded in making her feel very dowdy. She hadn't made any particular effort with her clothes. She was going on to work, she reasoned, and she was still angry with Damon. She wanted him to understand that she wasn't going to get all dressed up to impress him. She was wearing one of her endless shirt-blouses, blue this time, buttoned high, a plain navy skirt, and flat tan moccasins. Everything was polished and neat, but not exactly glamorous. Her beige-blonde hair was pulled back in the usual elastic band, but she had made one small concession to the occasion and tied a ribbon round it. Her skin glowed without any artificial aid, and her fine hazel eyes sparkled with a mixture of nervousness and temper.

Damon was waiting for her, sitting on a small gilt chair in the vestibule reading the business section of the morning newspaper, his long legs stretched out. He looked utterly composed, which added fuel to Philippa's fury. He was wearing a dark grey suit with a grey and white striped shirt. His wine-coloured tie was silk, and his gleaming black shoes looked as if they were handmade. He fitted perfectly into the plush atmosphere of the restaurant, while she felt decidedly out of place, but she swallowed hard, straightened her already ramrod spine, and allowed him to usher her to their table.

Once the meal was ordered, a simple one since neither ate heavily at midday, Damon leaned back in his seat and looked at her approvingly.

'You have an excellent virtue in a woman, Philippa, a rare one too.'

'I can't think what it can be. My beautiful nature, no doubt.'

'I don't know anything about that yet. You seem a pleasant-tempered young woman, though I suspect you could be difficult if you chose. I was talking about your punctuality. You walked through the door on the dot.'

'I make it a point to be on time for business appointments,' she said grimly. Damon's face became expressionless.

'Business, of course,' he agreed. 'I trust it meets with your approval if I get my lawyer to draw up a separation agreement, rather than offer you a lump sum before the ceremony. It seems in better taste that way. I'll finance the wedding, and pay for your new clothes, of course. I'll also deposit a nominal sum in your account for spending money during your stay in Crete,' he looked at her unsmilingly, 'does that suit you?'

She felt intimidated by his cold blue eyes, but stared unflinchingly into them and replied,

'The ... er ... agreement—it doesn't have to be complicated, does it?'

'Just details about the divorce.' Philippa gave a giggle of nervousness. 'Does the idea of divorce fill you with amusement?' His eyes were like flint.

'N-no. It's ... well, it's a bit odd discussing divorce when we're not even married yet.'

His expression did not change.

'Odd? I would say depressing. Not depressing for us, however, since this is only a business arrangement.' He glared at her.

'Sorry, but it's all rather strange,' Philippa remarked quietly, and a strained silence fell. 'When do you want me to start?' she asked after a moment.

'Start? Start what?' He gave her a look that bordered on contempt.

'Being married ... I mean, when do you want to have the wedding?' She was beginning to feel like a perfect idiot.

'In about two weeks.'

'So soon?'

'In a register office, of course,' he continued as if she hadn't spoken, 'and no guests, just two witnesses.'

'Do we have to have *anyone* there?' she asked glumly. This wedding was beginning to resemble a visit to the dentist rather than the most important day in a girl's life!

'It's the law,' he replied. 'I thought of asking my uncle. Do you have someone for a second witness?'

'I only have my sister. I told her about ... about us last night,' she added.

'Excellent. I'll organise it, then.'

The waiter arrived with their food—cold salmon for Philippa, and curried shrimps for her 'fiancé'. She picked away at the tender pink fish without appetite.

'When am I going to meet your sister?' Damon suddenly shot at her.

'M-meet Martha?' Philippa's appetite grew even smaller. This was a confrontation she hoped to delay as long as possible. 'Do you *have* to meet her before the wedding?'

'She'll think it a bit odd, won't she?' he countered. 'Or aren't you close?'

'Oh, we're very close. We share a flat.' And she thinks we're madly in love, she added silently, and if she meets you, and sees how cool you are, heaven knows what she'll think.

'Could you and your sister have dinner with me tomorrow night?' Damon's resonant voice broke through her thoughts.

'What?'

'Could I meet your sister tomorrow night ... Saturday ... for dinner?' he continued. 'In a restaurant, Philippa. I'm not asking you to cook for us.'

Philippa looked at him suspiciously; was he laughing at her?

'I'm sorry, Mr Everett, not tomorrow night. We're busy.'

'You are?'

'Yes. Martha's giving a dinner party. For fifteen people,' she added bitterly.

'You're helping her—is that it?'

'You could put it like that.'

'Well, I'll drop by for coffee,' he smiled broadly, and went back to his lunch with gusto. Philippa was thrown into immediate confusion.

'Er ... no ... that is ... Mr Everett, I don't think that would be a very good idea.'

'Why not?' he asked reasonably.

'Well . . . er . . . these are all young people . . . that is
. . . even *I* don't know them very well. You'd be bored
and . . .' she floundered.

'Don't be so stupid, Philippa! You talk as if I was
doddering. Which reminds me, I don't even know
how old you are.'

'Oh, I'm getting on,' she said seriously, 'I was
twenty-seven last month.'

She had never seen him laugh before, but now she did.
She looked at the strong column of his throat while he
tilted back his head and roared, causing several waiters
to look in the direction of their table, making her pink
with discomfort. At last he stopped, and taking a
handkerchief from his pocket weakly wiped his eyes.

'I'm delighted I amuse you so much!' she protested
indignantly. 'Believe me, it's not funny for a woman.
Twenty-seven's very close to thirty.'

'And thirty-nine's very close to forty,' he countered,
'and that's what I'll be on my next birthday. So it
seems that we're a couple of old crocks tottering
towards matrimony. Except that you look about
sixteen, and I feel far from an old crock. In fact, you
may find your young friends aren't as intimidated by
me as you seem to think they will be. Now stop being
silly, there's a good girl, and tell me your address.'

After she had mumbled it, and he had copied it into
a slim leather address book, he leaned his arms on the
table and looked full into her concerned face.

'Don't worry, Philippa, I won't drink my coffee out
of the saucer and disgrace you.' His voice was full of
laughter, so on the strength of his good humour she
decided to try and prepare him for Martha's possible
attitude towards him.

'I told Martha about you . . . us . . . last night, Mr
Everett, but . . . but I didn't tell her the full details of
our . . . our arrangement. She . . . er . . . thinks . . .'

'Very wise,' he interrupted her stumbling. 'Our contract has nothing to do with anyone else.'

'It's not exactly that, Mr Everett . . .' How on earth was she to explain the 'madly in love' part? She was panicky that Martha would make a remark about his supposed passionate love for her, and she wasn't sure how he'd take it, his moods seemed so mercurial.

'I think you should stop calling me Mr Everett,' he said. 'My name's Damon, you know.'

'Yes, of course . . . Damon.'

'That's better. Do you want dessert?'

'What?'

'Do you want something sweet to end the meal?' he said patiently.

'No. No, thank you, just coffee, please.' This in spite of the fact that she had a sweet tooth. She was about to try to explain her lie to Martha again, when he forestalled her.

'I presume you're interested in seeing what Athena looks like before you actually meet her?' He produced a photograph from a snakeskin wallet. It was a head-and-shoulders shot of a smiling dark-haired teenage girl, posed against a wall that was a mass of red oleander blossoms. There was a sliver of dazzling blue sea to the side of the picture.

'She's very pretty,' Philippa commented.

'She's the image of her mother,' he answered, taking the photo and looking at it tenderly before replacing it in the wallet. 'Athena and her mother were very close. Closer than is usual with most mothers and daughters. There were . . . circumstances . . .'

His expression became guarded and Philippa sensed that he had drawn down a shutter on the subject. It would be useless to pursue it further.

'Where was the photograph taken?' she asked. 'It's so bright and sunny. It can't have been taken in England.'

'No,' the shutter lifted a fraction and he gave her a smile, 'it was taken last year in Crete. Athena spent part of the holidays there with one of the teachers from her school. It's taken from the lower garden of my house.'

'Oh, you have a house in Crete, then?'

'One that was left me by my mother—yes. I hope you'll like Crete, Philippa—do you know Greece at all?' Damon enquired.

'No. I've never been abroad.'

'Naturally it's my favourite island,' he went on, 'but it's different from the other islands—harsher, less touched by European influences. But beautiful—very beautiful.'

'I'm looking forward to seeing it,' Philippa said formally, 'and to meeting Athena.'

Abruptly his mood changed. Glancing at his watch, he said briskly, 'Before I forget, this is your ring,' he held out a small blue leather box.

'Wh-what is it?'

'Why don't you open it and find out? It won't bite.' He pushed the box into her reluctant hand. 'Open it, Philippa, I haven't got all day.'

She pressed the clasp and the lid flew open. Inside was a magnificent sapphire ring, surrounded by a cluster of diamonds. She gasped and closed the box with a snap.

'Aren't you going to put it on?'

'I . . . I can't! I didn't expect . . .'

'To get an engagement ring,' he finished for her. 'We have to do things properly, Philippa. What would people think if a man in my position didn't give his fiancée a ring?'

What a fool I am, thought Philippa. This is all part of the front we're putting on, and I'm behaving as if it meant something.

'I shall of course return it when . . . when we split

up,' she said primly. The waiter brought coffee at this moment, and Damon dismissed him and poured them both a cup before answering her. When he measured the cream carefully into his cup she became aware of his strong male hand holding the silver pitcher, the nails manicured and well shaped, a sprinkling of dark hairs showing on his wrist below the cuff of his shirt.

'That will all be spelled out in the contract,' he said levelly. 'You'll have the use of all the family jewellery as long as you're my wife, of course.' She hadn't thought in terms of 'family jewellery'.

'Is this ring a family heirloom?' she asked.

'Not that one, no. I bought it for you this morning. Don't you like it? I can always change it for something else.'

She re-opened the box and took out the lovely ring, holding it to the light. It shone like blue fire.

'It's beautiful! I've never had anything so grand. Not even as a loan,' she added hastily.

Damon suddenly lost patience.

'Stop dithering, for heaven's sake, girl! See if it fits. I've a million things to do. I can't waste much more time away from the office.'

Philippa coloured bright red, slipped the ring on to the third finger of her left hand, and said,

'It fits perfectly. Do forgive me if I keep forgetting that I'm still an employee.'

He looked at her obliquely.

'I hope you don't intend to behave like my employee during our marriage,' he said. 'The whole purpose of this endeavour is to present a unified front of connubial bliss to the world at large. Any subservient behaviour on your part would wreck the whole plan. Quite apart from the fact that it would sicken me,' he finished cryptically.

She took a sip of black coffee to give herself time to collect her scattered wits, then setting the cup back on its saucer, she spread her left hand on the table and looked thoughtfully at the ring gleaming on her finger.

'There is one thing I must get quite straight, Mr Ever . . . Damon,' she said.

'Yes?'

'This "connubial bliss" part. It's quite understood that . . . well . . .'

'Well?'

She gave him a look of hatred. He wasn't even trying to help her! He surely must understand what she was trying to say. 'You specified that it would be a marriage in name only. I would like that put into the contract, please.' With hauteur she took a gulp of hot coffee and choked on it.

Damon handed her a glass of water with every appearance of solicitude.

'If you feel it's necessary to include it in the contract, I've no objection,' he said, 'but I assure you you're quite safe.'

Philippa winced from this insult, and considered flinging the water into his set face, but at that moment the waiter arrived with the check, and by the time he had left Damon was on his feet, all affability again, and somehow she was being helped into her raincoat and was standing outside in the light spring drizzle, her future husband towering beside her.

'Do you have your car, Philippa?' he asked.

'Yes. I have to shop this evening, so I need the car.'

'Of course. I can't offer you a lift, then.'

'No, thank you.' She glared at him, his cruel jibe still rankling. When he leaned down and kissed her quickly on the cheek she nearly fell over with surprise.

'Till tomorrow, then. Don't lose your ring in the flour bin!' His quick grin transformed him from an immaculate business man into a mischievous small boy. He left Philippa standing motionless on the pavement, with passersby milling around her, looking curiously at the tall girl who mumbled to herself, 'I'm mad . . . quite mad, to be doing this!'

She took Damon's ring off when she arrived at the maisonette where she was to work that evening; and she decided to leave it in its leather box when she got home later that night. She didn't relish any more scenes with Martha, and one look at that gorgeous sapphire would provoke one, she knew. But Martha was out when Philippa got home. There was a scrawled note pinned to her bedspread.

'Please wake me 10 a.m. Playing tennis Eric 11 a.m. Will be home late tonight. Don't wait up. Martha.' It seemed her kid sister had forgotten the request for help for the dinner party, but that was nothing new.

Philippa doubted she could do anything *but* wait up for Martha, since she had so much to think about, but the moment her head touched the pillow she went out like a light and didn't even hear her sister come in.

She woke early on Saturday and crept out of the apartment without waking Martha, merely leaving the alarm clock set for ten o'clock close to the sleeping girl, with a note propped against it saying she'd gone shopping. She remembered she had told Martha she would be shopping for her trousseau this morning, so she headed for a boutique in Richmond that she liked, and spent a pleasant hour buying herself some clothes. She would need things for Crete, she reasoned. She bought a full skirt of bright mauve and purple cotton, not her usual style at all, and a matching mauve silk shirt. To go with this she purchased some flat sandals, strips of purple leather that set off her well-shaped feet. She also splurged on a pair of white linen slacks to go with an emerald and white striped cotton blouse she couldn't resist. Her final extravagance that morning was a white one-piece swimsuit that she had to admit would look stunning once she had a tan.

She mused about these purchases over coffee and wondered why she hadn't bought her usual navy or beige skirt for summer. It must be the ring, she thought, it doesn't look as good with dull colours, and that influenced me.

The rest of the day was a scramble. She bought a ready-cooked ham, something she'd never done before, and masses of vegetables for salad. Arriving home, she found Martha's usual shambles—her bed unmade, a dirty coffee cup and plate on the kitchen table, clothes everywhere. This gave Philippa a slight sense of satisfaction, since she was feeling unreasonably guilty about the ham, and she felt cleaning up this mess absolved her a little.

She dashed around and put potatoes on to boil for potato salad, and garnished the despised ham to dress it up a bit. As a sop to Martha, or to her own conscience, she made an elaborate dessert—a Bavarian cream, rich with out-of-season strawberries and lashings of whipped cream. By the time she had made the salad and set the table—extending it with boards covered with a double sheet, an invention of her own she had devised for parties—it was six-thirty, and still no sign of Martha.

Philippa had just got out of a hurried bath, pulled on her new mauve skirt and matching blouse and sandals, when the doorbell rang and Martha's first guests arrived. Philippa greeted them with her hair still damp, and streaming in honey-coloured disarray.

It was a young couple she hadn't met before. She gave them some wine and chatted until more people arrived, then she left them to entertain themselves while she combed her hair into its ponytail and wondered if she should phone the police about Martha. She was getting worried.

At seven-thirty the hostess arrived, apologetic and giggly. She was dressed in brief tennis shorts under her coat, and looked tousled and pretty. Accompanying her was a young man, also in tennis clothes. He was startlingly good-looking, and Philippa guessed that this was the fabulous Eric. He never took his infatuated gaze from Martha's petite figure.

'Hi, everybody! Sorry to be late,' Martha called out, then gave Philippa's new clothes a hard stare. 'What *have* you got on Tusker?'

'Part of my trousseau. Don't you like it?' said Philippa, suddenly selfconscious.

'Oh, the skirt and top are fine. I'm just not sure they're right for *you*.' Martha smiled sweetly, 'I'll just go and change. Dinner won't spoil, will it?'

'Unless the ham grows legs and walks away from the table it can wait for hours.'

'Ham?' In an undertone Martha muttered. 'I thought we were having lasagne?'

'And I thought I was having help!' replied her sister grimly. She raised her voice. 'Before you leave us, Martha, aren't you going to introduce your young man?' She was aware of the hapless Eric hovering unhappily.

'Lord! I'm such a scatterbrain,' Martha twittered, a pale ghost of her mother. 'Everybody . . . this is Eric. Eric, this is everybody,' and with a gay laugh she disappeared into the bedroom.

Philippa introduced the dazed Eric individually to her sister's guests and then went into the bedroom herself. She had just remembered her engagement ring. It might be cowardly, but this seemed a good time for Martha to see it. With this crowd around she wasn't likely to make a fuss, and besides, she wanted a private word with Martha before they joined the party. She had time to slip the ring on to her finger before Martha came out of the bathroom and started throwing clothes around in a frenzy of choosing which dress to wear.

'Martha, where the hell have you been? I've been worried sick!'

'Sorry, Tusker, we went to the dearest little place for tea, and I just forgot the time.'

'You could have phoned.'

'I could have, but I didn't!' Martha yanked a shocking pink nylon dress over her head and wriggled her way into it. 'Do me up, Philippa, will you?' Her eyes fell on Philippa's left hand. 'Where did you get that . . . that *rock*?'

Philippa didn't like the greedy expression that filled the younger girl's brown eyes.

'It's my engagement ring. Mr Ever . . . Damon gave it to me yesterday. It's nice, isn't it?' she added placatingly, noticing Martha's downturned mouth.

'*Nice?* It's gorgeous! How much did it cost?'

'I haven't the faintest idea,' said Philippa with distaste, 'and I've no intention of asking. Come on, Martha, we're neglecting the guests.' And she led the way back to the living room.

Dinner passed without incident. Martha seemed subdued, but there were enough people around to take the focus of attention away from her sulky silence.

Philippa tried to make conversation with the besotted Eric, but it was hopeless. Privately she thought him a dreary young man, handsome or not, and she suspected Martha would tire of this inane devotion before too long.

She had just served the dessert to admiring murmurs, even Martha rousing herself from the sulks enough to say, 'Ooh!, Tusker, Bavarian cream . . . lovely!' when the doorbell rang. Philippa laid aside her serving spoon and wondered if the sudden pounding of her heart was visible through the thin silk of her new blouse.

'Who on earth can that be?' queried Martha.

'It's Damon. I forgot to tell you, he's coming for

coffee,' answered Philippa, amazed that her voice sounded quite normal.

'Who's Damon?' asked a guest.

'My sister's beau,' shrilled Martha. 'I haven't met him yet. Goodness knows what he's like.'

'Well, now you're going to find out,' said Philippa, going to the door. And you'd better mind your manners, little sister, she thought. I don't think Damon Everett takes kindly to bad behaviour.

She opened the door. It was always a shock when she saw him again to realise just how tall and broad he was. She found his solid frame reassuring. It was the first time she had seen him in casual clothes. The beige suede jacket and whipcord slacks made him look younger, and the maroon and beige checked shirt and silk ascot tied casually round his muscular throat gave him a jaunty air. He carried an enormous bunch of violets which he handed to Philippa. They smelled of spring.

She was so confused by this unexpected gift that she stood holding the flowers, her attractive nose buried in their fresh blossoms for a full minute before she thanked him for them. Then, pulling herself together, she said,

'These are lovely, Damon. But you really shouldn't have bothered. I don't expect you to bring me things, you know.'

He took this remark in his stride.

'Isn't it usual for the prospective bridegroom to bring his bride flowers?' The sound of his voice, smooth as liquid honey, sent a shiver of pleasure right through her body. She was so surprised by her reaction that she became even cooler.

'I wouldn't know, never having been a bride before. Besides, I hardly think these customs apply to us.' She faltered under his black look. 'I mean, our situation isn't particularly . . . romantic. You mustn't feel I expect you to do romantic things, like bringing me flowers.'

'Throw the damn things away if they cause you so much embarrassment,' he said savagely. 'I thought you'd enjoy them. Most normal women would.'

There was an awkward pause, which Philippa filled by burying her nose in the violets again, while Damon glared angrily over her head. After a few moments of silence he sighed and said,

'Why don't I go out and come in again, and we can start all over.' This broke the tension between them, and in spite of herself she giggled.

'There's no need. They must think it peculiar that we're spending so long in the hall. You'd better come in now.'

'They probably think we're billing and cooing like any engaged couple,' he said, 'so an extra minute won't confuse them. You're looking very nice, Philippa,' he went on, 'or will my paying you a compliment throw you into another rage? Like my gesture with the flowers.'

She coloured. 'Of course it won't. This is a new outfit,' she added unnecessarily.

'It's very attractive,' he assured her. 'I'm glad to see you've dropped the habitual mourning.'

'Mourning?'

'All those black and navy things you usually wear—very drab. This is a great improvement. I was going to mention it, but you've saved me the trouble.'

He was always doing this, Philippa thought crossly—behaving nicely, then spoiling it with a cutting remark. She never knew what to expect with this man.

'I'll go out and burn my entire wardrobe after coffee,' she said bitterly, 'then you won't have anything to complain about.'

Damon smiled goodnaturedly. 'Don't count on it. Are we having our coffee here in the hall?'

'Hardly,' she said with all the hauteur she could muster. 'Now, come in and meet my sister and her friends.' She led the way into the dining room.

A hush fell over the group when Damon entered, and Philippa was aware that it was not only his size which caused this, but the natural aura of authority he possessed. Martha's friends eyed him with respect.

Martha sat at the head of the table, a spoonful of whipped cream half way to her mouth. Her dark eyes widened as she took in the forceful face and piercing blue eyes of her sister's future husband, and she put her spoon, the cream untasted, back on her plate.

'Damon, this is my baby sister Martha,' said Philippa.

He approached the staring girl with a smile, and Philippa noticed that he had very nice teeth, white and even.

'I'm delighted to meet you, Martha. I hope we'll become good friends.' He enveloped her tiny hand in his powerful one. Still Martha did not say a word. Philippa broke the silence.

'Why don't you introduce Damon to your friends, Martha, while I put these in water?' She held up the violets and hurried to the kitchen, praying that Martha wouldn't make a scene. Besides, she didn't want to be absent too long. She might have to deflect the conversation, if Martha started making references to Philippa's fib of the previous night.

Jamming the violets into a large tumbler, she scurried back to the party. Damon was sitting at the table now, and the young people were laughing at something he'd said. Even Martha was smiling. Philippa heaved a sigh of relief. So far so good, she thought; it might be all right after all.

'Everybody ready for coffee?' she asked with forced

gaiety to mask the tension she was feeling, and proceeded to pour from the tray on the sideboard. One of the young men helped by passing cups around the table. Heaven forbid Martha should do more than play the gracious hostess at her own party!

'I congratulate you, Tusker,' her young sister's voice cut through the chatter and she turned to Damon. 'I think it's so clever of Tusker to have found someone her own size. Usually she towers over people.'

Damon looked puzzled.

'I don't understand. Who ... or what ... is Tusker?' he asked.

'Didn't Phil tell you her nickname? She's always called Tusker at home. Mummy named her that.'

'Why?'

'Because she's so big, of course. "Tusker" means she's like an elephant.'

Damon's honey-smooth voice became dangerously level. 'I fear your mother's knowledge of natural history was deficient,' he said. 'Elephants have wrinkled grey hides and lumber around like oversized battleships. Your sister is as graceful as a gazelle, and I've never heard of an elephant with skin like silk and beautiful golden eyes.'

Philippa stared at him in astonishment. She was not aware that he had ever noticed her eyes. The look Martha gave him was frankly hostile.

'But she *is* huge,' she said unpleasantly, 'you must admit that.'

'I admit no such thing. Your sister is *tall*—a very different thing from being "huge".'

'Well, I'm so small, and Mummy was too, and ...'

'It's hardly Philippa's fault she was brought up with midgets,' Damon countered equably.

Martha's jaw dropped, and Philippa waited with trepidation to see what *that* would provoke. Mercifully one of the other girls asked her when the wedding day was to be, and further discussion about Philippa's nickname was averted.

'I . . . I'm not sure,' Philippa answered her. 'In about two weeks, I think.'

'Two weeks to the day,' Damon broke in. 'We leave for Athens after the ceremony. I was going to tell you later,' he added to Philippa.

'Thanks. I might want to wash my hair,' she replied bitterly. This wedding day was not remotely like her dreams. But this was a business arrangement, she told herself, and had nothing at all to do with the romantic world of weddings these young people were talking of.

This reminded her again of her boast to Martha about being 'madly in love', and she sent out a silent prayer that nothing would be said. She would die with embarrassment if it was mentioned in front of Damon. Meanwhile the chat about the coming wedding went on. The idea of a honeymoon in Crete seemed to cause quite a stir.

'It's a working honeymoon,' Damon explained. 'I have to work while we're there.'

'I'm surprised you don't have a conscience about all your projects,' Martha said nastily, and Philippa's heart sank. It was apparent Martha had decided she disliked Damon and was out to bait him. However, her victim seemed quite undisturbed. He smiled at his future sister-in-law.

'A conscience? Why?'

'Building monstrous luxury hotels all over the place, and spoiling the countryside.'

'It's obvious you don't understand the purpose of my work at all.' He turned to Philippa. 'Does she, Pippa?' The surprise of hearing herself addressed so intimately by that velvety voice caused her to stutter like an idiot.

'N-n . . . no, I . . . I . . .' Damn him, she thought, to

hear him one would think he cared for me! His eyes were resting on her now with a gentle, amused look. His eyes are such a dark blue, she thought. Suddenly aware that she had been looking intently into those dark-fringed eyes for quite some time, she looked away in confusion. He was the most unsettling man she had ever met, and she felt irrationally annoyed with him for putting on such a good show in front of Martha and her friends.

He continued talking to Martha. 'I do more than just finance the building of my hotels,' he explained. 'I act as a liaison between the architect and the builders. I make it my business to see that everyone connected with the running of the hotel is satisfied with their working conditions. And I have a particular concern for the local people. If you study our track record I think you'll find that we've not spoiled any of the towns or villages. On the contrary, we've provided work for the locals, and contributed to the community as a whole.'

'So *you* say. I still think you're a . . . a sort of parasite . . . destroying everything.' Martha's mouth was curving downward in that discontented droop Philippa had come to dread. 'I think people like you should be stopped by law!'

'Well, I wouldn't suggest that to the people of Chania, you wouldn't be very popular,' he replied. 'They're staking a lot on their new hotel.'

Martha's new boy-friend now asked a question.

'How are you going to manage with the language? If you use local people it's not likely they'll speak English, is it?'

'Most unlikely,' Damon agreed, turning his broad shoulder on Martha's thundery face. 'Fortunately I speak fluent Greek. I learnt it from my mother.'

'From your mother? Are you half Greek, then?' The question blurted out of Philippa before she had time to think. Martha caught the slip in a flash.

'You mean you didn't know, Tusker? Your own fiancé? For heaven's sake!'

'I . . . er . . . forgot,' her older sister said lamely. Her cheeks flaming, she cursed herself for her stupidity.

Martha's eyes were alive with malicious curiosity.

'You *forgot*! I don't believe you, Tusker. You wouldn't forget a thing like that!'

Scarlet with confusion, Philippa looked helplessly at Damon.

'You have to excuse Philippa,' he said. 'I've been so busy trying to sweep her off her feet I've not given her a moment to remember anything.' He put his large well-shaped hand over Philippa's. The touch of his warm skin on her palm sent an unexpected shiver of delight from the nape of her neck down her back, so that she hurriedly tried to pull her hand away, but he held it firmly, and leaned forward to look intently into her hazél eyes. 'I didn't want to give her time to change her mind. When a man's lucky enough to find a girl like Philippa he shouldn't waste time with a lot of past history. We'll have plenty of time to find out about each other once we're married.' He smiled at the assembled company. 'And now if you'll excuse us I'm going to take her away for a while. We've things to discuss.' He released her hand at last and stood up. When she continued sitting looking up at him speechlessly he took her arm and pulled her to her feet, then let his arm fall familiarly round her waist. For the first time in her life Philippa felt tiny, the top of her silky blonde head just reached his shoulder. She tried to tactfully ease herself out of the arc of his encircling arm, but he merely tightened his hold on her slender waist, so she gave up and tried not to look selfconscious.

'Don't wait up for your sister, Martha,' Damon said wickedly, 'we've quite a lot to talk about.'

'B . . . but the washing-up . . .' Philippa murmured.

'I'm sure Martha will see to it tonight,' he said genially, ushering Philippa towards the door.

Martha raised her voice and said venomously, 'I presume you *are* coming home tonight, Phil? If not, don't forget your toothbrush!'

The crowded room became silent. Martha glared defiantly at Damon and her sister. Damon's hand dropped from Philippa's waist and he took a step in towards Martha. Philippa looked at his face. All trace of joviality was wiped from it. His well defined mouth was set into a grim line, and his eyes were cold as steel. Philippa felt sorry for her little sister, whose attitude of defiance was visibly wilting in the face of Damon's anger. When he spoke his voice was low, which was more menacing than if he had raised it.

'Consider yourself lucky there are people present; otherwise I'd put you over my knee and give you the spanking you deserve,' he said to the amazed Martha, whose petulant face turned dull red. Philippa broke in hastily.

'It's all right, Damon—Martha was just making a joke. She didn't mean anything by it.' It was one thing to have her reputation protected, but he was a stranger, and she felt a rush of family solidarity. She also felt that this charade he was playing was beginning to get out of hand.

'If it *was* a joke, which I frankly doubt, it was a joke in very poor taste. However, I won't embarrass your company by insisting on an apology *this* time. But you keep a civil tongue in your head in future, young lady. Understand?' He gave Martha a long hard stare, then turned to Philippa, who was becoming more furious with him each second. 'Come, Pippa.' He put a masterful arm through hers and imperiously swept her from the room. When he opened the hall cupboard for their coats they could hear the hum of conversation start again in the dining room. Philippa snatched her

raincoat angrily from his hand, before he had a chance
to help her on with it. Once they were out in the soft
April night she turned on him like a wildcat.

'How dare you say such things to my sister! Making
her look like a fool! How dare you! Just who do you
think you are?' Her hazel eyes flashed fire, her cheeks
were pink with indignation.

'I know exactly who I am. I'm your fiancé.'

'My *fake* fiancé,' she snapped.

His look became remote.

'As you wish. However, I still feel an obligation to
protect you, even if there's no ... no affection ...
between us.' He took hold of her arm in an iron grip
and proceeded to partly guide, partly pull her to a
silver-grey Jaguar XJ that was parked by the curb.

'I'm perfectly capable of protecting myself, thank
you,' said the livid Philippa. 'I don't need you to do
it!'

Damon let go of her arm, she could still feel the grip
of his fingers on her flesh. He opened the car door and
stood aside for her to get in, but she stubbornly stood
on the pavement, rubbing her bruised arm.

'I'm sure you're capable, Philippa. But your spoiled
brat of a sister was being obnoxious, implying you're
little better than a trollop . . .'

'You didn't have to make a scene,' she repeated
obstinately.

'Perhaps what Martha implied is true? Perhaps you
make it a practice to stay out all night when you go out
with a man? I wouldn't do that,' he added quickly,
catching her wrist as she aimed a slap at his brown-
skinned cheek. To her total humiliation she burst into
tears of rage.

'How d-dare you! How d-d-dare you!' she gulped.
'You're nothing but a bully! First Martha and now
me!'

Damon fished in his pocket and produced a clean

white handkerchief which he handed her. 'If you have to hit someone, Pippa, why on earth didn't you hit your sister? She's the one who insulted you. Now blow your nose like a good girl and get in the car.' He gave her a friendly push in the direction of the automobile.

The interior of the car smelled of leather and a fragrance that she was beginning to recognise as Damon's aftershave. Dabbing at her cheeks with his handkerchief, she could have sworn that his eyes were tender when he looked at her tear-stained face, but she told herself not to imagine such nonsense, and blew her nose loudly to help pull herself together.

Well, that's torn it, she thought. I've ruined the whole thing before it's even started. The knowledge that this arranged marriage would probably be off now filled her with a depression that was not entirely due to the loss of a holiday in Crete. She was startled to realise that she was beginning to find Damon's company stimulating. She liked his massive shoulders lowering over her, the scent of him. She found the web of lines at the corners of his dark blue eyes attractive, and when he gave her one of his tender smiles her heart lurched like a ship in a storm. He maddened her! There were moments when she could hit him—just now, for example—but his rugged virility and male animal charm was beginning to captivate her. Careful, girl! she warned herself, you're liable to fall for this man, and that will never do. To guard herself against such folly she sat primly in the burgundy leather car-seat, her long shapely legs stretched out before her, and her whole body pushed against the car door, as far from Damon as possible.

He drove fast and with assurance. She stole a glance at his profile, which was visible in the passing street lights. His hair, which was crisp and curling in the damp April weather, was not quite as immaculate as usual. One lock fell over his broad forehead, giving him an air of a small boy, rather than his normal image of sober business executive. His firm mouth curved gently, and Philippa recognised that his full lower lip revealed a violence in his nature that his controlled behaviour hid. She would not like to be the focus of his temper, she thought, but to unleash the passion that she was becoming aware of, to feel that strong mouth on hers . . . this thought was so delicious that she sat straighter in her seat and turned her head away from him before saying.

'I apologise for my behaviour just now. I'm sorry I tried to slap you . . . I feel dreadful about it . . .'

'Maybe you're just sorry you missed?' he grinned at her.

'Please don't joke, Damon—I'm *serious*. And of course I realise that our mar . . . our *arrangement* can't possibly take place.'

He didn't look at her but slowed the car a little.

'What on earth are you talking about, Pippa?'

'Our marriage,' she said flatly. 'It was obvious tonight that it would be too difficult to . . . to keep up that sort of pretence . . . I nearly gave everything away to Martha with my stupid surprise about you being half Greek.'

'That's why we're going to spend time indoctrinating you. Starting tonight over a drink at a club I go to sometimes.' The car accelerated again.

'A club?' she queried.

'At Kew. More like a private pub really. I think you'll like it.' He glanced at her briefly. 'You can wash your face and generally repair what little damage your crying jag has caused. As for our wedding being off, you can put that idea right out of your head. I'd take a very dim view if you reneged on our contract now. You're not a quitter, surely, Philippa?'

'It's not that at all,' she replied, 'but it's so difficult with Martha. You obviously don't like her . . .'

'I wouldn't say she's wild about me either,' Damon said laconically.

'You see? It makes everything impossible.'

'Don't be silly, Pippa. I'm not marrying Martha, I'm marrying you. And we'll be in Crete from the moment we're married. And think how happy Martha will be when she discovers our brief . . . liaison . . . is over. She'll crow with satisfaction—tell you what a lucky escape you've had, how she sensed from the moment she met me that I was nothing but trouble. We *have* to get married, just to give your sister the joy of saying "I told you so" when we get divorced.'

Philippa didn't particularly enjoy the turn this conversation was taking, so she remained silent for the remainder of the drive.

The club was located in an old house on the Kew towpath. Damon parked the car and led her through a shadowy garden heavy with the scent of lilac. They entered the oak-panelled hall and Philippa went to wash her face. Gleaming chrome taps gushed hot water, and an antique basket held an assortment of expensive soaps to choose from. There were thick face towels on an oak rack, and opened bottles of French colognes for the use of the guests. She chose a lilac-perfumed soap because it seemed to blend in with the scent of the garden outside. She combed out her beige-fair hair and decided not to tie it back in her usual ponytail, but left it loose, falling like a glossy curtain on her shoulders.

The sitting room, where Damon was waiting for her, was a quiet oasis after her emotional turmoil. Situated on the first floor, it had old fashioned bow windows that leaned out over the river Thames. Pools of light from peach silk shaded lamps created cosy islands with groupings of chintz-covered armchairs and low oak tables. They sat by one of the windows, and Philippa could hear the whisper of the river as it slid under the dark arches of old Kew Bridge. The ancient Thames, murmuring on its journey to the sea. She sank into the soft chair with a sigh of pleasure. She could feel the day's tensions melting away. It was so peaceful and companionable with Damon in this pretty room, the scent of lilac drifting in from the garden, Damon sitting opposite, his strong face softened by the golden lamp light. She could almost make believe that this was a room in their own home, and they were a married couple, spending an intimate evening together, in perfect harmony. Watch it, girl! she cautioned herself, that kind of daydreaming leads to trouble.

A white-jacketed waiter brought a tray and set it on the table beside Philippa. 'I thought you might be hungry, Pippa, so I ordered us a snack. I hope it's what you like,' Damon said.

It looked delicious, and Philippa found she was hungry. She'd not had time to eat much at dinner, as usual she'd been far too busy making sure the guests were fed to think about herself. Damon had ordered pâté, a sharp Cheddar and fine Cheshire cheese, with several kinds of biscuits. There was a dish of fruit, and a damson flan with a side bowl of cream. She tried a slice critically (she made a good damson flan herself). It melted in her mouth, the cream yellow and slightly tart, the way of authentic Devonshire cream. They drank brandy, and she poured them both cups of aromatic coffee.

Damon grinned at her. 'You look like a cat who's just polished off a particularly rich dish of cream!'

'Very apt, since that's just what I've done.'

'Well, now that you're feeling rested and satisfied let's begin your education ... your education regarding me, that is. Ready?'

'Ready! I now know that you're part Greek.'

'Yes. My mother was Greek, from Crete. My father

was English. We lived in Crete, but I went to school in England. And I spent many happy holidays in Cornwall with my father's family. My father's brother will be coming from there for our wedding.'

Involuntarily Philippa exclaimed, 'Oh, lord!' The wedding loomed like an ordeal to be lived through.

'He would never forgive me if I got married without inviting him. He and my niece Athena are my only living relatives now.'

'But if it's only a marriage of convenience is there much point to him being there?' queried Philippa.

'He won't know it's a marriage of convenience, as you put it. And I'm not going to try and explain it to him. He'd never understand.'

'I'm not sure any normal person would,' Philippa brooded. 'Won't he be very upset by the divorce?'

'I hope not. I'll just say we were incompatible, and hope he'll take it in his stride.'

'What about Athena? Will she take it in her stride too? Or do you plan to tell her our bizarre secret?'

'There's no need for anyone outside of the two of us, and my lawyer, to know,' Damon insisted, 'I prefer to keep it that way.'

Philippa recognised the stubborn set of his jaw, and didn't pursue the subject. 'Will your niece be at the wedding too?' she asked.

'No. She's at school in Athens. She joins us there the day after our marriage. Then we sail to Crete together.'

'Will she like me, do you think?' It suddenly occurred to Philippa that she and this unknown Greek child might heartily dislike each other at sight. Then Damon's neat little scheme would be flawed.

'I see no reason why she shouldn't. In any case, she has many friends in Athens and in Crete. I don't expect you to spend every moment with her. She's a reasonable girl, so I don't foresee a problem.' This was not quite the reply Philippa had hoped for, so she tried another tack.

'Since Athena is your ward I presume she's an orphan.' Damon didn't answer immediately, and when he did his voice was curiously flat.

'Athena's father is still alive. He left my sister when Athena was a baby.' He took a sip of brandy before continuing, 'My sister and my parents were killed in a car crash four years ago, and I've had custody of my niece since that time.'

Philippa noticed that the harsh lines that ran down to his mouth were more pronounced. His eyes looked bleak. She longed to take his hand, to show sympathy, but his expression was so forbidding she didn't dare.

'I'm sorry, Damon, I had no idea.'

'How could you have?' His blue eyes met her hazel ones. 'I was very close to my family. And Athena and her mother ... they worshipped each other. It was natural, I suppose, for Helen to shower her daughter with love. Athena was all she had left after her ... after her husband deserted her. And Helen loved him, God help her. Sometimes in the night I'd hear her crying ... my little sister who was so gentle, so trusting ...' his voice broke, but he quickly recovered himself. 'I wanted to hurt him the way he'd hurt her. I would have killed him with my bare hands!'

His eyes were opaque with hatred, and Philippa felt a frisson of fear. This urbane man kept a tight rein on his emotions, but they were closer to the surface than she had supposed.

He gave himself a mental shake and said in a lighter tone, 'Fortunately for him I could never find him. But you see how important it is that Athena has some upbringing. She's been through so much in her short life, poor child. And I'm so busy, I don't have the time to devote to her. She needs a woman to share things with, to talk to. The scars of her loss will never fade, but you could help to heal them, Philippa.'

His sincerity gave her the courage to ask, 'What about your scars? Have they healed?'

'Me? Oh, I'm fine as long as I have my work.' His voice regained its resonance. 'I love my work. I'm fortunate, since I don't *have* to earn money to live comfortably.'

'You don't?'

'No. My family are quite well off.' He smiled at her. 'The world will say you've made a good match, Pippa,' he finished ironically.

'Why do you keep calling me Pippa?' she asked.

'It's my new nickname for you. A vast improvement over "Tusker", don't you think?'

'It sounds like an old apple core,' she said. But secretly she was pleased that he had taken the trouble to find a pet name for her.

'It's from *Pippa Passes* by Robert Browning. Browning's one of my favourite poets.'

'You like poetry?' She was delighted.

'I don't find your astonishment very flattering,' he teased. 'Do you suppose I read only financial reports and hotel plans?'

'Of course not. But it's such a coincidence. Browning's one of my favourite poets too!' She bubbled with enthusiasm, '*Pippa's Song*. Isn't that "God's In His Heaven, all's right with the world"?'

'That's one of the songs. But not the one I was thinking of.' He suddenly became very businesslike, which prevented her questioning him further. 'I've arranged for you to see my lawyer on Monday morning at ten. He has the settlement drawn up for you to sign.'

'Monday at ten is fine,' Philippa replied soberly. The reminder that their coming marriage was strictly business was a downer after Browning.

'I trust you'll find the terms to your satisfaction,' said Damon.

She wondered why he had become so distant, almost as if he was annoyed to discover they shared similar literary tastes. He's more temperamental than Martha, she thought; what on earth am I letting myself in for?

'On Monday afternoon I want to take you shopping,' he went on. 'My firm's throwing an engagement party for us next weekend and you'll need suitable clothes.'

Philippa opened her long-lashed eyes wide. 'I think you've been so tolerant, Damon,' she cooed, 'allowing yourself to be seen in public with this frumpish beanpole.' She glared at him.

'I don't choose frumpish beanpoles to act the role of my wife,' Damon assured her.

'What do you choose? Trendy cooks?'

'Hardly trendy.' His contemptuous tone chilled her.

'This arrangement isn't going to work, Damon,' she said in a small voice.

'It will work very well, Philippa, if you'll just improve your self-image. It annoys me when you constantly put yourself down. You speak of your height as if you were a freak . . .'

'I feel like one sometimes!'

'Don't interrupt. You're a fool, Pippa. You're a very attractive girl, who could be beautiful if only you'd take the trouble to make something of yourself.'

'*Beautiful?*' she echoed, stunned.

'Certainly. After we've bought you some pretty dresses, and shoes with decent heels on them, you'll see.' His black mood was evaporating. 'You should wear clothes that have fluid lines to show off your excellent figure. And I don't want to see your glorious hair scraped back in that hideous tail thing any more.'

'Hideous?' she echoed lamely.

'It looks very nice loose, the way it is now.'

'I can't wear it loose when I'm cooking,' she said defensively.

'You don't cook twenty-four hours a day Pippa,' he smiled at her disarmingly.

Now that his anger had passed he seemed utterly approachable and she decided to unburden herself.

'I get scared, Damon, when I think about Crete, and being your ... your hostess. I'm frightened that I'll let you down. You need someone with poise, and ... glamour ... to be your wife, even your makebelieve one.'

Damon leaned across the table and looked deeply into her eyes, and she noticed how long his dark lashes were. She must have been blind not to have noticed before how disturbingly handsome he was. The whites of his eyes had a slight blue shade which made the irises the colour of indigo.

'It's true, Pippa, that you're not glamorous.' She could have wept at this home truth! 'But that's easily fixed, if glamour is your aim. I flatter myself that I make sound decisions. I know I do in business, while my experience with women has been limited.' (Of course, there *must* have been women in his life, so why did this depress her?) 'As for poise,' he continued, 'I've never met anyone as young who has so much natural dignity and poise. I believe in you. All I ask is that you believe in yourself.'

Philippa examined her short unpainted nails in an attempt to disguise her confusion. She was extraordinarily conscious of his closeness, the texture of his skin, the well-kept sweep of his dark hair. What's the matter with me? she thought. This man is my business partner. Why should I feel weak with pleasure because he pays me a few compliments? It simply won't do.

She deliberately shattered the moment by making a flippant remark. 'My goodness, Damon, you're so dramatic! It's easy to tell you're half Greek—no Englishman would be caught dead being so emotional!'

His face grew stony, and she felt awful, knowing she'd hurt his feelings, and he had been saying such nice things! But she mustn't let him know what a powerful effect he had on her.

'It offends you? My foreign blood?' His mouth was a set line.

'There you go again!' Her forced laughter was as brittle as glass. 'Taking everything so *seriously*! Of course it doesn't offend me. It has nothing to do with me. I don't even think about it.' She stretched her pretty mouth in an unnatural smile—a smile her eyes did not mirror.

'As you say, it has nothing to do with you. And now I think it's time to end this tête-à-tête.' Damon got up from his chair without another word and strode off to get their coats. Philippa followed, miserably aware that she had wrecked the evening. But better to destroy one evening than let him guess that his good opinion caused her such pleasurable turmoil.

They drove back to Hammersmith in silence. Damon drove much too fast, and the atmosphere in the car was one she could have cut with her favourite meat cleaver. He screeched to a halt outside her front door, but left the engine running.

'I won't see you in, Philippa. You might think it too emotional of me to walk you to the door.' He looked like a hurt small boy. She couldn't let them finish the evening this way.

'Damon, I'm sorry, I didn't mean to upset you. I was thoughtless.' There was no denying the sincerity in her tawny eyes. He waited a moment before he answered.

'Ah, Pippa,' he sighed, 'we're living a lie, and that's always difficult. Even a lie for the most honourable of reasons takes its emotional toll. You were quite right, neither of us should take this situation too seriously.' His tone became brisk. 'Now, goodnight, Pippa. I'll see you on Monday at the lawyers. Have a good rest tomorrow.'

The car was gone the moment she had clambered out of it, before she had a chance to say, 'Goodnight, and thank you.'

She entered the flat, deserted now by Martha and her friends, and miraculously tidy. Damon's suggestion about the washing-up had apparently been heeded.

Philippa felt let down by Damon's sudden departure. Last time they had parted he had brushed her cheek with his lips, and she realised she had been looking forward to a similar farewell.

She *must* discipline herself to continue picturing him as her employer only. Not as her fiancé, or her husband, but simply a man who had hired her for a limited time, to play a role in his life for business purposes. It would be fatal if she started getting romantic ideas about her boss.

'He's only my boss. He's only my boss,' she muttered to herself while she waited for sleep. But in spite of this valiant attempt, her last waking memory was his honey voice saying, 'I believe in you . . .' and it continued, over and over again, in her dreams.

# CHAPTER THREE.

MONDAY's meeting with Mr Farjeon, Damon's lawyer, was uneventful. Damon was there to co-sign the documents, dressed in a navy blue suit, and looking less boyish than the other night. He seemed to have recovered his good humour completely, and smiled cheerfully when Philippa walked into the office.

Mr Farjeon was a stooped white-haired man of about sixty-five, Philippa judged, and he obviously found the situation strange. He was very cool to Philippa, regarding her suspiciously from under untidy white beetling eyebrows. He made no bones about the fact that he intended to protect his client from any fortune-hunting females. Silently he handed her a copy of the agreement to read. Damon sat opposite her, looking quite at ease, as if he had this kind of contract drawn up daily.

'That clause you requested, Pippa,' he said, 'concerning the non-sexual nature of our relationship—it's been included on page two.' He regarded her coolly.

'Thank you.' Her cheeks flushed under the combination of Damon's amused look and his lawyer's disapproving gaze.

When she reached the paragraph that dealt with the sum she would receive when the marriage was annulled she protested,

'Damon, this is ridiculous!'

Mr Farjeon broke in before Damon could reply. 'What exactly do you object to, Miss Kenmore?' His faded old eyes behind his glasses were hostile.

'Why, the amount mentioned here—it's absurd!'

'I think not,' he went on in his precise manner. 'I must say I think my client has been generous—more than generous, I might go so far as to say foolish in the amount set out in the agreement.'

'Exactly!' Philippa flashed the older man a brilliant smile. 'Foolish is exactly the word for it,' and turning to Damon she said impulsively, 'It's far too much, Damon. I don't want anything like that. In fact I'm not sure I want any settlement at all.'

'Don't be silly, Pippa. You're going to lose a whole summer's work by coming to Crete with me. I must reimburse you for that at least.'

'But I wouldn't make anything like the amount you're offering,' she insisted. 'I'd feel badly. I won't accept it, Damon. If you want me to sign this agreement, that clause has to be changed.'

'You have a very prominent chin when you get that stubborn look on your face, Pippa. Did you know that?'

'You change the amount of the settlement to a reasonable sum, and I'll change the angle of my chin,' she countered.

During this exchange the frost in Mr Farjeon's manner started to thaw, and he regarded Philippa with friendlier eyes. 'If I might suggest, Mr Everett,' he offered, 'perhaps Miss Kenmore could tell me how much she earned during the past year. Would you say fifty per cent of that amount would be fair?'

'Yes,' said Philippa.

'No,' said Damon.

'Come, come, Mr Everett. It's what Miss Kenmore desires.' The old man threw her a positively conspiratorial look; obviously she had won him over. She told him the amount, and he wrote it down on a notepad.

'All right,' Damon conceded. 'Fifty per cent . . . and a new car. The one she drives now isn't roadworthy,' he added in an aside to Mr Farjeon.

'That's not true! My Mini's perfectly O.K.,' protested Philippa hotly.

Mr Farjeon held up an admonitory hand. 'Shall we leave the question of personal gifts out of the contract?' he suggested. 'I advise you to settle the matter of the ... er ... vehicle in question between yourselves. Now I have altered the amount of the settlement to the agreed fifty per cent, so it only remains for you to sign.' He handed Philippa a pen, and so brought the argument to a close.

Once they were out on the street Damon took her arm and swung her towards him.

'Pippa, I mean it—about the new car. I worry about you driving around in that ramshackle old tin can of yours.'

She fought twin emotions—hurt pride that he found her car—a second-hand one she had scraped and saved for—an 'old tin can', and growing delight that he felt concern for her. Resolutely she smothered her delight.

'We can't all afford to drive Jags, you know,' she said shortly.

'I wasn't proposing to buy you a Jaguar. Just a newer version of your present jalopy,' he gave her arm a friendly shake. 'Come on, Pippa! It's not good manners to keep on refusing my gift. What's the matter? Afraid I'm after your virtue?'

She turned bright scarlet and tore from his grasp. 'I wouldn't be stupid enough to think *that*,' she snapped.

'Nor likely to fall from grace if I was,' he answered quietly. She remained silent. 'Look, Pippa,' he said, 'let's forget this whole business about the car for the moment and get on with the rest of the day. I'm starving, aren't you? Let's have an early lunch and then start on your shopping spree.' He smiled down at her, the web of lines around his eyes crinkling goodhumouredly. 'What do you say, Pippa? Lunch?

Before I drop at your feet in a swoon from lack of food.'

His mood was infectious and she grinned back. 'You don't look as if you're wasting away, but I *am* hungry—so all right, lunch it is!'

They drove to the Prospect of Whitby, one of London's historic old pubs. Philippa had never visited it before, but she had read an article about it in a magazine. It enchanted her, with its sagging old floors and blackened oak beams, which Damon had to bend almost double to avoid hitting. They had been hewn from solid trees in the reign of Elizabeth the First. Although the district now consisted of slums and warehouses people came from all over the City to lunch in the ancient saloon bar with its creaking floors and leaded windows that had looked out over the Thames since the sixteenth century.

Damon ordered a half pint of draught ale for himself, and a shandy for Philippa. They ate fried whitebait, minute silver fish the size of a matchstick, fried crisp golden brown and eaten with the fingers, several fish to one delicious mouthful. This was accompanied, traditionally, with slices of thickly buttered brown bread. After a platter of fish they left to have coffee and pastries at a smart café in Knightsbridge that Damon knew. There he ordered black coffee for himself, and a generous china cup of foaming café-au-lait for her.

Philippa agonised happily over the three-tiered pastry cart loaded with a multitude of rich cakes, and finally chose a sugar-glazed mille-feuille, bursting with fresh whipped cream. She lingered over it, savouring each bite like a child being treated by an indulgent uncle. When she had wiped away the last flaky crumb from her mouth she became aware of Damon's blue eyes smiling at her. She smiled back ruefully and said,

'You've guessed my guilty secret!'

'And what's that?'

'My terrible sweet tooth. That cake trolley is my idea of paradise!'

'You're not going to stop with just one, are you?' Damon asked. 'The éclairs are famous here.'

She giggled happily. 'I couldn't, Damon, I just couldn't!'

'In paradise there's no such word as "couldn't"!'

'Are you Lucifer to tempt me?' she teased.

'I hope you never see me as the devil, Pippa,' he said, his face suddenly serious. 'However,' he brightened, 'if I can't tempt you now we'll come back at tea-time for the éclair.'

'If I go on indulging like this I'll have to buy all my new dresses at least two sizes larger!'

'Don't be silly, Pippa,' he said loftily, 'you're not the type to get fat. Besides, you're tall enough to carry a little extra weight.'

'You're a dangerous man to be around,' she said. 'At this rate I'll soon be the size of a blimp!' But in her heart she meant this warning for herself, and it had nothing to do with weight. She was so happy with Damon today. Being with him was a heady mixture of ease and excitement. And this she knew was dangerous.

Damon had chosen a boutique in Chelsea for their shopping, but when they reached the door Philippa felt a sudden panic. It was the type of shop she had often peered into, but never had the nerve to enter. There was always one exclusive garment cleverly arranged in the display window with no price tag visible, and she always knew ahead of time that she could not afford the kind of prices those exclusive clothes inevitably commanded. She now hung back outside the elegant shiny black door.

'What's the matter, Pippa?' Damon asked.

'I don't think this is . . . my kind of shop.'

'Why not? I'm not in the habit of buying women's clothes, but my sister used to buy her dresses here, and she was a very smart woman. That's why I chose this store.'

'That's just it, Damon. Your sister was fashionable, I'm not. I couldn't begin to match up—I'm not the type.'

'What rubbish are you talking now?' he replied, his voice sharp.

'One must be practical,' Philippa said levelly, 'one can't make a silk purse out of a sow's ear.'

'A *sow*! Good God, Philippa!' He exploded with irritation. 'What is this fixation you have with animals? First an elephant, now a pig! If you must compare yourself with the animal kingdom choose more attractive specimens. Now come on—I haven't got all day.' He opened the door and bundled her through before she had time to protest further.

Inside all was gleaming creamy rose satin and crystal-shaded lamps. Philippa's flat-heeled walking shoes sank into white carpet that felt ankle-deep. They were greeted by the proprietress, a woman of middle age, who spoke with a slight French accent, and looked as if she had stepped out of the current issue of *Vogue*.

Apparently they were expected. Damon introduced her to this glamorous creature, who turned out to be friendly and courteous. This was a pleasant surprise to Philippa, who had expected condescension from so polished a being.

'I've some business close by, Pippa,' Damon said. 'I'll leave you in Madame Martine's capable hands and come back in two hours. Will that be all right?'

Panic overwhelmed Philippa for the second time in several minutes. How would she know how much to spend? How many dresses was she supposed to buy?

As if he could read her mind he continued, 'You're to buy everything you need. Remember we'll be doing a lot of entertaining, so you'll need dinner and evening dresses. Sporty things too, and things for the beach. In fact anything that takes your fancy. Have a nice time.' He was at the door in two strides, then he turned and gave her one of his rare sweet smiles. 'And Pippa—don't be "sensible" about your choices ... promise?'

After he had gone Madame Martine ushered her into a change cubicle so spacious it seemed to Philippa to be almost the size of the bedroom she shared with Martha at home in Hammersmith.

'Now that I've met you, Miss Kenmore,' Madame Martine said, 'I can better judge what style will best suit your particular build and height.'

Philippa's heart sank. 'I suppose I'm difficult to fit,' she said dismally.

Madame Martine looked puzzled.

'On the contrary, you will show off my clothes particuarly well. I only wish all my customers had your figure, it would make my job much easier, I assure you!'

Philippa wondered if this was clever sales talk, but the woman sounded quite sincere. So she brightened up, and kicking her shoes off stood, slim and straight in her slip, to start the pleasant business of choosing new clothes.

The following two hours flew by. Madame Martine knew her job and each dress she produced fitted perfectly. There was one particular evening dress, of wine silk, that Philippa fell in love with. It was cut on the lines of a Grecian dress, and moulded itself to her slender hips, falling low at the neck revealing more of her well-formed breasts than she usually showed. She revolved slowly in front of the triple mirror, and lifted her heavy beige hair to get the effect of a piled hair-do.

'That is a very good style for you, Miss Kenmore.' Madame Martine's voice startled her, she had been so absorbed in her scrutiny. 'If I might suggest a particularly good hair-stylist,' the woman continued, 'he would trim your hair just a little, so that it would fall attractively when loose, and would be easy to put up when you wanted.'

Very soon Madame Martine had taken Philippa in hand. Not only had she phoned the hairdresser for an appointment, she had made suggestions about make-up, and told Philippa what kind of shoes she should buy.

'Now, Miss Kenmore, I think we have seen enough of the day and evening clothes,' she said finally. 'Let me show you some very fine nightdress and peignoir sets that have just arrived from Paris.'

Philippa came down to earth with a crash. It was all very well for Damon to foot the bill for clothes she would be using as part of her job, but what she wore to bed was something he would never know. Her serviceable cotton pyjamas would do.

'I . . . I won't be needing any nightdresses, thank you, I don't wear them . . . that is . . .' The woman's brows raised quizzically, and Philippa turned bright red. 'I wear pyjamas,' she mumbled.

'Not on your honeymoon, surely, my dear!'

'Honeymoon? Yes . . . well, perhaps a nightie . . . and a dressing-gown too, I suppose,' she muttered, ready to die of embarrassment. She chose a filmy peach nightdress with a matching robe, and frivolous satin slippers stitched with pearls, without putting up a fight.

Now it was time for her to decide which dresses she would choose out of the dozens that hung around the walls of the fitting room.

'I must have this,' she said, fingering the wine silk dress lovingly, 'and maybe the white strapless one we tried on last.'

'Mr Everett gave instructions that you were to take everything that looked good on you,' Madame Martine told the startled girl.

'Bu-but the *cost*!'

'That's all taken care of, Miss Kenmore. Mr Everett will settle the account. He particularly stressed that you were not to be bothered by any of the financial arrangements.'

At this moment they heard the sound of the front-door bell, and Damon's voice filtered through the rose silk curtains of the fitting room.

In a dream Philippa put on her grey flannel skirt and cotton blouse, which now felt very dowdy. Damon arranged with Madame Martine to have the luxurious pile of multi-coloured clothes delivered to Philippa's flat the next day. In a dream she followed Damon to the car, and sat silent while they drove back to the café, where she silently drank tea and ate the promised chocolate éclair.

He looked at her, concealing an amused smile. 'So quiet, Pippa! Has the thought of emerging from your chrysalis stunned you?'

'Not exactly,' she replied, 'although I do feel as if I've had a head-on collision with Santa Claus! It's very pleasant. I feel a bit guilty, though.'

'Guilty? What on earth for?'

'To get so much, when poor Martha . . . What's the time, Damon?' she asked abruptly. He told her, and saying, 'Hang on a minute!' she dashed out of the café, leaving him sitting, bewildered, at the table.

She had noticed that next door was a small boutique, and now she tore in just before it closed and purchased an expensive silk scarf in the shocking pink colour that Martha loved so much. She was back at their table within minutes, only slightly out of breath.

'I thought you were going to turn into a pumpkin,

Philippa,' he said drily, 'or should I say an elephant?'
She flushed and poured them both more tea.

'I'm sorry, Damon, but I wanted to get Martha
something. Just to make her feel . . . less left out.'

Damon did not look pleased. 'Left out of what?' he
queried. 'It's your wedding, not hers. Why shouldn't
you have new clothes? It's usual.'

'But so many . . . and such heavenly ones! She's
bound to feel upset, and I don't want a scene.'

Damon frowned and his eyes turned cold. 'I don't
understand you, Philippa. You work your fingers to
the bone, and when a chance comes along for you to
have some pretty things and enjoy yourself for five
minutes, you spoil it all by feeling guilty. And all
because that self-indulgent sister of yours might be
jealous!'

'You hardly know my sister, so I fail to see how you
can accuse her of self-indulgence,' said Philippa hotly.

'You don't have to know her to see that,' he
retorted, 'it sticks out a mile. She constantly expects to
be catered to, and it's obvious you're fool enough to
do it.'

Philippa began to lose her calm. She was particularly
maddened since honesty forced her to admit there was
truth in what he said.

'I may be a fool,' she hissed, 'but at least I'm a
generous one!'

'There's no virtue in that,' he sneered. 'Buying her
off simply means you're a coward, besides being an
idiot. And you'll doubtless go on letting that selfish
brat take advantage of you for the rest of your life!'
Philippa gasped at the ferocity of his attack.
'However,' he continued icily, 'it's not my affair if you
choose to ruin your life.'

Furious, she eyed him. 'As you say, it's none of your
affair,' she retorted. 'Now, if you've finished your
character assassination of my sister I'll leave you.' She

got up from her chair and picked up her purse. 'Thank you for a pleasant day . . .'

Damon was on his feet and beside her in seconds, pushing her back into the chair and flinging her purse to the floor. 'I'm not ready to leave yet,' he said, his voice hoarse with temper. 'When I've had a second cup of tea I'll drive you home, not before. I would remind you that I'm calling the shots in this . . . *partnership*. You'll leave when I'm ready, not before.'

If the cake knife hadn't been so blunt she would have thrown it at him! As it was she contented herself by picking up her handbag, rising to her feet again with all the dignity she could muster, and removing her engagement ring and placing it on the white tablecloth in front of his plate.

'I've decided I don't like the terms of this *partnership*, Mr Everett,' she said. 'I'll arrange to have the clothes returned. Thank you again for a most interesting experience. Goodbye!' And she stalked out of the café, uneasily aware of the goggle-eyed interest of the waitress.

She strode along in the twilight, blinking back angry tears. Her long legs took her at a rapid pace, but she had no idea where she was going.

How dared he! she thought; he doesn't even know Martha. What gives him the right to criticise her like that? And calling me those names! Who does he think he is? Carrying on as if the way I run my life is any of his business. It's not as if he cared for me, she went on to herself bitterly, it's obvious I mean no more to him than an efficient secretary . . . or *cook*.

'Pippa!' He was right behind her, but his voice was no longer harsh. He caught hold of her arm and stopped her in mid-flight.

'Let me *go*!' She was unreasonably angry, furious with herself that the sound of his voice made her heart leap with joy. Furious, knowing she would have been sick with disappointment if he had not followed her.

'Pippa, please! Don't be angry. I'm ... I'm sorry.' This apology, so uncharacteristic for so proud a man, stopped her in her tracks.

'You had no right to talk like that about my personal life—no right at all!' she said fiercely. 'I would remind you that we have a *business* arrangement. *Strictly business*, nothing more.'

He dropped her arm and regarded her somberly.

'I'm aware of that, Philippa. You're quite right, it was unpardonable interference on my part. But I do ask you to consider renewing our ... agreement.' His eyes in the dying light seemed black they were so dark, and the lines that ran down to his mouth looked deeper than before. 'If you won't think of me ... and there's no reason you should ... at least think of Athena. It will be impossible for me to find a replacement at such short notice. We do have a legal contract,' he added softly.

Silently Philippa started walking again, but this time she walked back the way she had come and he fell into step beside her. A light April rain started to fall and the streets gleamed wetly in the lamps.

'Well, Pippa?' he asked after a while. She stopped and faced him. He looked as remote as he had in the past sitting at his kitchen table waiting for her to finish clearing away the debris of one of his dinner parties.

'Very well,' she said, 'since I can see it would be difficult for you in the circumstances. And for the sake of your niece.' She was grateful that it was dark now, since she could not fully meet his eyes knowing in her heart this was not the whole reason.

'Then let me return your ring that you so dramatically threw back at me,' said Damon lightly. He took her unresisting hand in his and slipped the sapphire back on to her finger. Instead of it making her feel happy she felt a grey mist of depression steal over her. The setting was so romantic—the big, handsome man, putting a magnificent engagement ring on the third finger of her left hand, the London street lights shining on his dark hair that was a little damp with rain.

And it's all a sham, she thought sadly, it's just a front for a convenient business transaction.

They were both silent on the drive back to Hammersmith. Damon arranged to pick her up the following Friday for his company's combined engagement and farewell party, but he didn't make any mention about seeing her before that. As usual he kissed her lightly on the cheek, so that for a brief moment she felt his warm mouth brush her face. Then she was alone on the rain-slicked pavement, watching the red tail-lights of the Jaguar disappear in the darkness.

# CHAPTER FOUR

THERE was no sign from Damon for the rest of the week. Philippa tried to discipline herself not to start with anticipation every time the phone rang, not to let a note of disappointment creep into her voice when someone else was on the line. But she found it increasingly difficult. She was forced to admit that she missed him—that without his overbearing presence her life was flat and drab, that she would rather be with him, even if they were at odds, than be without him.

However, she had plenty to occupy her. There were clients to be contacted, business appointments to be cancelled, and all the exacting details a prolonged absence from home and work entailed.

She went to the hairdresser's as Madame Martine had arranged, and spent an intoxicating couple of hours being clipped and combed by a languid young man who was extravagant in his praise of her heavy blonde mane, and sent her out of the salon with hair two inches shorter, that fell in a soft curve around her face and lay curling gently on her shoulders. He instructed her how to dress it in other styles, and she bought an array of multi-coloured combs and hairbands for the purpose.

After a visit to a shoe shop, where she purchased several pairs of high-heeled shoes and sandals, she went to a boutique specialising in cosmetics, and was shown how to make up her eyes so they glowed golden, and her thick lashes curled back like the petals of a flower.

On Friday morning there was a phone call from

Damon's private secretary. At first Philippa thought he was waiting to be put through—but no, he was 'very busy', his secretary, a Mrs Hicks, informed her.

'Mr Everett says he'll be sending a car for you and your sister at seven this evening, Miss Kenmore ... for your engagement party at the Savoy Hotel.' When Philippa remained silent she added, 'And Mr Everett said to remind you that it's semi-formal, not full evening dress.'

'Tell him I'll put my tiara back in mothballs!'

'What?'

'Nothing. Thank you for calling, Mrs Hicks. Tell Mr Everett we'll be ready at seven as arranged.'

'I will. We're so looking forward to meeting you tonight, Miss Kenmore. Goodbye.'

Philippa was bitterly disappointed that Damon hadn't taken the trouble to speak to her himself. But he had included Martha, which was nice of him, in the circumstances. She phoned her at the travel agency, and to her surprise Martha seemed eager to accept. After she had hung up a small cloud of anxiety settled over Philippa. She hoped her sister's sudden willingness to co-operate wasn't prompted by a desire to make trouble in front of Damon's staff. But there was nothing she could do, except cross her fingers and hope for the best!

She took her time getting ready for the party, brushing her ash-blonde hair till it crackled with vitality, and swung, a honey-coloured bell on her shoulders. She made up carefully, applying a hint of bronze shadow to her eyes as she had been shown, so that her eyes had the brilliance of topaz when she looked into the mirror. She wore a dress of fine wool challis, long-skirted and coloured palest pink, like the heart of a seashell. The bodice was drawn across her breasts in a deep vee, and ended in a sash tied on one side of her waist, the ends falling softly into the unpressed pleats of the skirt. The effect was stunning in its simplicity.

She was sitting in the bedroom applying a second coat of pink nail polish to her fingernails when Martha arrived home. Philippa looked up from her absorbing task straight into Martha's astounded face. Carefully replacing the brush in the bottle, she waved her wet nails in greeting.

'What on earth are you doing, Tusker?' asked her sister.

'My nails. Nice colour, eh?'

'But you never wear nail polish.'

'I do now. I must grow my nails longer, though.'

'That won't be practical,' Martha said acidly, 'they'll chip when you work.'

'I don't plan to be working—at least not in the kitchen.'

Martha's eyes grew hard. She looked at her sister's glowing face. 'Have you cut your hair?' she asked.

'Just a trim. I like it, don't you? It's going to be very easy to manage this way.'

'And you're wearing make-up, aren't you?' This sounded accusatory.

'Mm-hmm. You'll have to give me some tips,' Philippa said diplomatically, 'you're so good at make-up.'

Martha didn't deign to reply at once, instead she looked askance at her sister's feet. 'You're not going to wear those shoes, are you?' she demanded, glaring at Philippa's pretty new taupe suede sandals.

'Certainly. Don't you think the colour's right?'

'It's not the colour, it's those heels. You'll tower over everyone!'

'I won't tower over Damon.' Philippa tilted her chin obstinately and changed the subject. 'The bathroom's free, Martha, you've got forty minutes to make yourself glamourous.'

Martha started pulling clothes out of the bedroom cupboard and hurling the rejects all over the room.

'Isn't that dress you're wearing rather plain, Tusker?' she queried.

'I don't think so,' Philippa replied serenely. 'It's not a full dress party, remember?'

'Still, I should have thought you'd wear something with a bit of sparkle.'

'I leave the sparkle to you, Martha.'

'I guess glamour just isn't your style,' Martha agreed smugly, pulling her silver dress over her head.

'I guess not.' Philippa repressed the treacherous thought that the silver dress looked overdone—an effect that was not lessened by the addition of long rhinestone ear-rings and bracelets.

A chauffeured Daimler picked them up on the dot of seven, and drove them to the Strand through streets filled tonight with the intangible quality of a London spring—a subtle mixture of exhaust fumes, lilac blossom, and the damp scent of the river Thames.

The statue of Peter of Savoy stood guard over the entrance of the Savoy Hotel as it has since the place was built. Damon was waiting for them in the art-deco lobby that was decorated with small flags of many nations. The board bearing the information about the daily Atlantic Crossings still hung in its place of honour, although in this jet age it only boasted one departure the following week.

When Philippa slipped out of her light silk coat— 'You'll need a coat for those cool Greek evenings, Miss Kenmore,' Madame Martine had assured her— she was gratified to notice Damon's look of approval. But it was to Martha that he spoke.

'I'm very glad you came this evening, little sister-in-law,' he said. 'Let's bury the hatchet, but not in each other. Agreed?'

'I'm happy to come to your party,' Martha cooed,

sweet as sugar, her eyes glittering with hatred, 'but why the Savoy? I thought you'd want to show off in one of your own hotels.'

'The one hotel I own in London is very quiet and small. Which may come as a surprise to you, Martha,' he grinned, 'since you seem to think I only put my money into monstrous edifices. In any case, I love the Savoy. The fact that it was created by Richard D'Oyly Carte, and some rooms have the names of Gilbert and Sullivan's operas, gives it a raffish charm that appeals to me. And I feel the history of the Savoy is appropriate for an engagement party. Look!' He led them to a plaque set in the wall which read, 'Here in the palace of the Savoy, Peter, Count of Savoy, lodged the many "beautiful foreign ladies" whom he brought in 1247 from the courts of Europe before marrying them to his wards, a large number of rich young English nobles.'

'It's a charming idea,' acknowledged Philippa, 'but it doesn't apply. I'm not a "foreign lady".'

'*Beautiful* foreign ladies,' he replied, taking her arm, 'and foreign to the Greek half of me, so don't quibble.'

'Thank you.' She accepted the compliment, and then added softly, so Martha couldn't hear, 'Since those marriages were arranged too, I suppose there is a link.'

Before he could answer they were joined by a small dapper man whom Damon introduced as Michael Wilson-Parkes, manager of the hotel, and a personal friend. Michael took both Philippa's hands, and holding her at arm's length said firmly,

'She's lovely, Damon, you lucky fellow. She's absolutely lovely!' still holding her hands he turned to her. 'You *are*, my dear, you're absolutely breath-taking!'

Philippa, scarlet with embarrassment, made an inarticulate noise, and was saved by Damon, who introduced Martha, whose face was sullen with resentment.

'Charming', said Michael, briefly nodding in her direction. He looked at Philippa again. 'If Damon wasn't a dear friend I'd ask you to jilt him this moment and run away with me.'

Philippa, aware of Martha's hostility, without thinking blurted out,

'I can't jilt Damon—we have a legal contract.'

The little man laughed delightedly and finally let go of her hands. 'And I wouldn't dare,' he said, 'not when Damon is so obviously very jealous,' for Damon was looking black as thunder at this exchange. 'I'm envious of your good fortune, Damon. She *is* so lovely.'

'And so *businesslike*,' Damon choked furiously. 'My bride is a business woman first and last.' He glared at Philippa, who smiled weakly at him.

'I'm not used to such extravagant attention,' she said, 'it unnerves me.' He gave her a look of ice from his piercing eyes and turned to Michael Wilson-Parkes.

'Our guests arrive at eight. We'd better get to our dining room. You have arranged for us to be in one of the private rooms?'

'Pinafore, old boy,' affirmed Michael, 'less far for Kasper to travel.'

'Good. You've arranged the head table for thirteen, then?'

'Your wish is our command, old boy. That's our motto. And now, you lovely creature,' he turned theatrically to Philippa, 'regretfully I must tear myself from your side, but don't despair, I'll return later, to drink a glass of champagne to your bright eyes.'

'What an ass!' Martha said rudely when he had gone. 'Are all hotel people like him?'

'Don't be fooled by Michael's manner,' said

Damon, 'he's no ass, believe me. And now if you'll excuse us for a moment, Martha——' He drew Philippa out of earshot, then turned on her. 'For God's sake, what are you trying to do,' he snapped, 'telling Michael we have a contract! Why not use the P.A. system while you're at it, and broadcast to the whole hotel!'

Philippa wished the thickly carpeted floor could have opened up and swallowed her. She went red, then white with emotion. 'I'm sorry, Damon,' she pleaded, 'but I found it so . . . embarrassing . . . coping with all those good wishes. When I know . . . we know . . . this arrangement has nothing to do with sentiment.'

'We also know you're being amply rewarded. I would appreciate it if you'd earn your money properly in future.'

The brutality of this helped her regain her composure, the injustice of it fired her own temper. 'You didn't mention anything about public engagement parties when we reached our understanding,' she reminded him hotly. 'Pretending to be your wife in Crete is one thing, being paraded before your friends and entire London staff is something else!'

Damon executed one of those characteristic changes of mood she was beginning to recognize. After a pause he grinned sheepishly, 'I'm sorry about the party, Pippa—my partners sprang it on me as a complete surprise. But I warn you, we'll get plenty of good wishes in Crete too, so you'd better get used to it. Now, our guests should be arriving any minute. We'd better get to our reception room.'

When the three of them entered the room named 'Pinafore' they found small tables to seat groups of eight dotted around a charming room, lit by cosy art-deco wall sconces, and a handsome central candlelabrum. The long head table was decorated with garlands of spring flowers, and laid for fourteen. But at one of the places, perched high on a silk cushion, sat a sleek black wooden cat, a napkin tied under his chin, and a complete place setting, including wine glasses, laid before him.

'Allow me to introduce you to Kasper the cat,' said Damon.

Philippa was delighted. 'He's gorgeous! Is he yours, Damon?'

'No. He belongs to the hotel. Whenever there's a dinner party for thirteen in any part of the hotel, Kaspar's invited to become the fourteenth guest. It's a long tradition.'

'How stupid,' Martha's voice was sullen, 'wasting good food on a dumb ornament!'

'He doesn't get any food,' Damon explained, 'but when each course is completed the appropriate items of cutlery are taken away from him. He lives over there,' he indicated the mantelpiece, 'so for this party he didn't have to travel too far.'

'I think it's a charming tradition,' Philippa said hastily, to prevent Martha making any more disparaging remarks. 'Thank you for arranging it, Damon.'

'My pleasure.' He inclined his glossy dark head ironically, but she was aware that Martha's ungraciousness had not gone unnoticed, and sent out a heartfelt prayer that her mood would improve.

In due course the guests started arriving—Damon's two partners, their wives, and the staff of his head office in London. There were about forty people in all, and Philippa attempted to spend the same amount of time with each, so no one would feel snubbed. Besides, she wanted to make up for her gaffe with Michael Wilson-Parkes.

She would have quite enjoyed herself if she hadn't been so anxious about Martha. She kept glancing in her direction, then saw to her relief, that one of the young unattached males in the party was devoting all his attention to her, and Martha was smiling again.

They sat down to a superb dinner—pâté maison, flavoured with cognac, lobster bisque, and a main course of Charollais steak, accompanied by delicious wild mushrooms, black as jet, and tasting faintly of perfume. Each course was accompanied by the correct wine, which Philippa drank sparingly, knowing she needed her wits about her for this first test on her new 'job'.

After the fruit and cheese had been cleared away the waiters carried in a handsome cake with the names 'Philippa and Damon' iced on the top, and a positive riot of sugared violets wreathed around them. When it was cut the interior seemed to consist almost entirely of whipped cream, with pieces of almond and apricot scattered through it. Champagne was served now, and toasts to the engaged couple were given.

This stage of the proceedings filled Philippa with discomfort. A naturally honest person, she felt like a cheat. She found it humiliating to sit beside Damon, smiling at the friendly faces before them, knowing in her heart that it was all a sham. When one elderly gentleman, in a rather long-winded toast to the 'happy pair', made a laborious reference to the possible 'patter of little feet', she wanted to disappear into thin air with mortification. She caught Damon's eye, and he made a tiny signal, raising his dark brows slightly in comical despair. This made her feel better.

At the end of the evening they were presented with a magnificent cut glass bowl, and again Philippa's cheeks burned with shame. Damon made a speech of thanks, witty and brief, in which he managed to be as unsentimental as possible without drawing attention to the fact. He drew the dinner to a close by suggesting they all head for the ballroom and dance for the remainder of the evening.

'We'll have to go too, to start things off,' he said to Philippa, when everyone was collecting wraps and getting themselves organised. 'You do dance, I suppose?'

'Of course. Do you?' She led the way to the old-fashioned elevator, inwardly praying she wasn't too rusty. It had been ages since she'd danced.

Damon had reserved tables for the party, and had arranged for champagne. And Michael joined them for the promised glass.

'May I have this dance with your beautiful bride, Damon?' he asked.

'You may not. She's all mine for the rest of the evening,' and Damon swept her on to the floor without another word.

Like many big men, he was light on his feet. He led her firmly, and after a few moments' concern, wondering if she'd be clumsy, Philippa relaxed and enjoyed the dancing. They danced well together. She shut out all the nagging thoughts about this strange alliance she was entering the next day, and gave herself up to the sensuous pleasure of the feel of his hand, so warm and strong, on her back, the thrust of his thighs against hers.

The music stopped. He didn't let her go, but stood still, holding her close, until the orchestra started another number. This dance was slow, and she found her head drooping towards his shoulder, to rest there voluptuously. With an effort she jerked it upright and pushed her body from his. Damon peered into her face.

'What is it, Pippa?' he murmured.

'We seem to be dancing awfully close.'

'We're an engaged couple. We must give the right picture.' He pulled her back against him once more and continued dancing, but this time she did not relax. She was aware of every movement of his well-muscled body close to hers. She imagined she could feel his heart beat. Worse, she fancied he might feel the pounding of her own tumultuous heart.

The music came to a close again, but this time he stepped away from her.

'We've created enough of an illusion,' he said harshly. 'I'll drive you home now.'

Philippa felt as though he had dashed cold water in her face; she forced her expression to remain neutral and followed him off the floor.

'Do you want to stay, Martha?' Damon asked, taking charge. 'You don't have to leave on our account.'

Martha yawned loudly. 'I'll come home too,' she said. 'This place isn't exactly jumping.'

'Suit yourself,' he replied indifferently. 'I'm taking Pippa home. I don't want a hollow-eyed bride at the registry office tomorrow.'

Damon drove them home in his Jaguar. They arrived at their front door, but Martha made no move to leave the engaged couple alone, and ignored the stern look he gave her. He reached into the pocket of his overcoat and drew out a flat box, which he handed to Philippa.

'These pearls belonged to my mother,' he said, 'I'd like you to wear them tomorrow.'

Philippa opened the box. The single strand of perfectly matched pearls glowed creamily against the velvet interior of the box.

'They're lovely!' she breathed. 'Look, Martha!'

Her younger sister gave a cursory glance at the proffered jewels. 'They're O.K. . . . if you like pearls.'

'You don't, I take it?' Damon asked.

'Pearls are for old ladies.'

'In that case I won't embarrass you with my wedding gift to you.' He smiled thinly, and holding up another box, lifted the lid to give them a brief glimpse of a delicate gold chain, from which hung a heart-shaped locket covered in seed-pearls. Snapping the box shut, he put it back in his pocket. Martha's face was a mask of fury.

Damon opened the door for the sisters, and made a point of seeing Martha disappear into the flat before he spoke.

'You managed splendidly tonight, Pippa.' He sounded like a boss at the end of a particularly difficult day at the office. 'I'm very satisfied that you'll fulfil your part of our bargain admirably.'

Just what every bride longs to hear on the eve of her wedding, thought Philippa wryly, but she schooled herself to give him a cool nod. 'It wasn't as difficult as I thought. I found myself quite enjoying the evening.'

'Yes? Well, once we get the legal part behind us, and get settled in Crete with Athena, it should be plain sailing,' he purred.

'The legal part? You mean the wedding?'

'Yes. Once we've passed that hurdle, we can relax.' His eyes were as blank as glass.

'Hurdle? Yes, I suppose that describes it pretty well.' As if I were a pony going over jumps tomorrow, she thought bleakly. 'Well, goodnight, Damon,' she forced herself to sound brisk, 'I'd better go in now, if you don't want me to have bags under my eyes tomorrow.'

'Goodnight, Pippa.' Once more she felt his lips brush her cheek, and he was gone.

Martha was climbing into bed when Philippa went into the bedroom.

'Lover-boy gone?' she asked.

'Damon's left, yes,' Philippa said mildly.

'That was a pretty crummy thing to do, with the locket.' Martha lay back, her petulant face pinched with temper.

'You were pretty crummy yourself, Martha. Why can't you be polite to Damon?'

'Because I hate him, that's why—I hate him!'

'I'd appreciate it if you'd be polite, just the same,' Philippa persisted. 'It makes it so hard on me when you go out of your way to be rude.'

Martha's set face didn't change, and Philippa was filled with unease about the next day. She sat on the edge of her sister's bed.

'Martha, will you promise me something?' There was no reply. '*Please!*'

'What?' said Martha grudgingly.

'Promise me you'll behave tomorrow. Don't shame me. Don't make a scene on my wedding day.'

Martha hunched her shoulders and scowled more than ever.

'If you won't promise I won't let you come tomorrow,' Philippa said firmly. 'I'll get another witness if I have to. I couldn't *bear* it if you made a scene.' The very thought of it made her blood run cold. 'For my sake, Martha? Please?'

'Oh, all *right*, Tusker,' Martha replied with bad grace, 'but I still think you're making a big mistake.'

Damon was right, Philippa thought, Martha will be delighted when we separate. She'll never let me forget that she warned me it wouldn't work. For a moment she wondered if her scheme to civilise her little sister was doomed for failure from the start. Well, it was too late to call it off now. And she had to admit that she didn't want to call it off. She wanted a summer with Damon. Even if one summer would have to last her for the rest of her life. She wanted it more than she'd ever wanted anything.

# CHAPTER FIVE

PHILIPPA KENMORE was married to Damon Everett the following afternoon. It was a simple civic ceremony. Outside an April wind blustered, chasing fat white clouds across an intense blue sky. It was a day buoyant with happiness, a day to make any bride's heart glad. Any bride but Philippa! She was filled with a sense of unreality. The plain gold band, so shiny and new, proclaiming to the world that she was indeed married, did nothing to banish this.

Things had gone well, though. Martha had behaved herself. She didn't murmur when she was given a plain chestnut-brown dress to wear for the wedding, chosen to complement Philippa's apricot wool suit.

Damon's uncle had turned out to be a darling. Colonel Richard Everett was a handsome gentleman of almost seventy-five. He had a straight-backed, military bearing, a shock of silver hair, clipped white moustache, and Damon's eyes, blue as sapphires.

He and Philippa had taken to each other immediately, but his enthusiasm about his nephew's marriage made Philippa feel more of a fraud than ever.

After she had signed the register—Philippa Kenmore, for the last time—they stood blinking in the wild spring sunshine. Colonel Everett turned to Philippa.

'Now, m'dear, you'll all come to my hotel for a glass of champagne.' He cocked a white eyebrow at his nephew. 'That agree with your plans, Damon?' When Damon accepted he went on, 'Good, good. Don't know what you can have been thinking of, Damon. Marrying a fine gel like this in such a hole in the corner fashion. Fine gel like Philippa deserves a *proper* wedding!' He glared at Damon.

'We wanted a quiet wedding, Uncle Richard.'

'Quiet? It was practically inaudible!' He glared again, then catching sight of Philippa's face he relented. 'Never mind m'dear,' he said, 'you're married, and that's all that matters when you're in love. Right?' He bundled them into a hired car. 'Brown's Hotel,' he barked at the driver, and turning to Philippa continued, 'Nothing matters when you're in love, eh, m'dear? And Crete's a lovely place for a honeymoon. Makes up for a quiet wedding.'

'A *working* honeymoon, Uncle Richard,' Damon interjected.

'What's the matter with you, m'boy,' answered his irrepressible relative, 'taking a working honeymoon with a beautiful bride like Philippa? Tell you what, m'dear,' he turned to the discomfited Philippa, 'if you get bored on your honeymoon, with that dull nephew of mine, just leave him, and come and visit me in Cornwall. I won't work while you're around, I promise you!' He leaned back in the leather car seat and roared with laughter until he started to choke. 'Oh, you'll love my house at Polperro,' he said, when he had regained his breath, 'won't she, Damon? And you too, m'dear,' he turned to the hitherto ignored Martha, 'you must come and visit me too. We're relatives, after all. Do you like the country?'

'I hate it,' Martha said shortly.

This took the ebullient old gentleman back a bit, and before he had recovered himself they had arrived at Brown's Hotel. The Colonel took charge at once, and guided them into its discreet interior. It was apparent he was known here. Like many country people he regarded Brown's as a 'home away from home' on his visits to London. And the traditional atmosphere suited him. They went into an elegant drawing room overlooking a quiet inner court. Colonel Everett then went into a huddle with an elderly waiter, and joined them after a few minutes, obviously very pleased with the result of this conference. He fixed a gimlet eye on Damon.

'You are the most inept bridegroom I ever met,' he said, 'I trust you'll do a better job as a husband. Fortunately they've plenty of champagne on ice, so your poor lady won't be forced to leave on her honeymoon without at least one toast to the bride.'

'I'd no idea you were such an authority on weddings, Uncle Richard,' his nephew teased. 'I don't recall you ever taking the plunge.'

'Never met the right gel. Not like you, m'boy.' He took Philippa's hand and patted it fondly. 'Forgive an old man, m'dear. When I'm happy I tend to go on a bit. Bear with me.' He beamed at her, and at the disgruntled Martha, who, Philippa could tell, was becoming restless at not being the centre of attention.

Champagne arrived at this moment, with a platter of smoked salmon, prawns, cold sliced meats, and the result of Colonel Everett's conversation with the waiter, a large iced fruit cake, decorated with a bunch of orange blossom.

'Uncle Richard, you're a genius!' Damon was obviously moved. 'Where on earth did you find the orange blossom?'

'Not me, m'boy, you must thank Brown's.' He poured them all glasses of the sparkling wine and started to make a toast, when Martha interrupted him.

'I'd no idea of the time, Tusker!' turning her back on the Colonel. 'I'll be late for my date if I don't leave now.'

'Leave?' The Colonel was horrified. 'You can't leave! You haven't even tasted your champagne.'

'I don't like champagne, any better than I like the country,' Martha said rudely.

Damon took charge.

'Let her go, Uncle Richard.' He rose to his feet. 'Goodbye, Martha. Thank you for taking the time to attend your sister's wedding.'

Martha wilted under his look.

'I . . . th-think . . . perhaps I could stay, for a few minutes more,' she stuttered.

'Certainly not,' Damon replied, moving to her chair and practically tipping her out of it. 'You mustn't keep your date waiting. I understand, Martha. I understand *perfectly*.' He looked at her with distaste.

'Well . . . er . . . goodbye, Tusker, and good luck.' Damon put his large hand under her elbow, and marched her to the door. 'Don't forget to write?' she managed to call before Damon hauled her away.

Philippa sat, white-faced and sick with shame. She couldn't look Damon's uncle in the eye. He'd gone to such trouble for them, and to have Martha behave so badly! She stared miserably at the champagne fizzing in her glass.

'I . . . I'm terribly sorry, Colonel Ever . . .'

'Now, m'dear, don't say another word. Young gels get upset at weddings sometimes,' he offered tactfully. 'You mustn't take it to heart.'

'But you've been so kind, Colonel . . .'

'Uncle Richard, m'dear.'

'. . . Uncle Richard, and . . .' The old man's gentleness brought tears to her eyes, which she hastily blinked away.

'Now, now, m'dear, no tears,' he said, 'not on your wedding day. I can't begin to tell you how happy you've made me today. I'm not a young man, and I didn't know if I'd still be around when Damon finally settled down . . . if he ever did. I'm glad he doesn't have to finish up a crusty old bachelor, like me. It's lonely, and I wouldn't wish it on him.'

Philippa sat, rigid with distress. If only he would

stop! He could have no idea how guilty he was making her feel. He took her hand again, the left one, where the new wedding ring gleamed at her reproachfully.

'Be good to him, Philippa. He's been through a lot these past years. Love him. He needs you, and your love.'

Mercifully at this moment Damon returned, his face impassive. He picked up his glass. 'You were about to make a toast, Uncle Richard,' he said.

'Yes, I was, m'boy. A toast to your lovely bride. Make her happy, Damon. I suspect she hasn't always had plain sailing.' His eyes, faded, but still so blue, looked deep into hers. 'God bless you, m'dear. God bless you both.' They all took a sip of champagne, then the Colonel leaned forward and kissed her lightly on the cheek. She smiled, in a private agony of humiliation. 'Well?' said the Colonel to Damon. 'Aren't you going to kiss the bride?'

'Of course I am, Uncle Richard.' He moved to her chair, and lifting her to her feet, put his arms firmly round her and kissed her full on the mouth. Philippa was taken completely by surprise. His kiss was angry, hard. His cruel mouth punished hers, bruising her lips. His arms crushed the breath from her body. She could sense his pent-up rage . . . at Martha? At himself perhaps, for putting them both in this ludicrous position.

Finally he let her go, and breathlessly she sat back at the table, forcing herself to give Colonel Everett a calm smile. Together she and Damon cut the cake. His hand over hers was like a vice.

She forced herself to swallow a few crumbs. It was very good, but it stuck in her throat like sand. Damon and his uncle began talking about some improvements Colonel Everett wanted to make to his Cornish house, and Philippa had a moment to reflect, bitterly, that the first, and probably only, kiss she had had from her husband had been one of hate, not of love. Damn Martha! she thought. The promise she had extracted from her to behave at the wedding should have extended to the wedding reception.

Finally it was time for them to leave for the airport. They left the Colonel standing on the steps of the hotel, looking forlorn and rather frail, in spite of his military bearing.

The bride and groom didn't speak until they were installed in the first class cabin of the aircraft that was taking them to Athens, then Damon turned to her.

'I owe you an apology,' he said. 'I'd no idea my uncle would behave like that. I know he's wanted me to get married, but I didn't realise he would be quite so enthusiastic.'

Philippa regarded her new husband coldly. 'You don't have to apologise for Colonel Everett,' she said, 'I think he's a darling. But I *am* furious that I have to lie to him, and hurt him eventually. I've never felt so shabby in my life.'

'When the time comes I'll tell him of our separation, and take all the blame, don't worry,' he answered cynically.

'Honestly, Damon!' Philippa's voice rose with exasperation, then she noticed a curious glance from the stewardess, and lowered it. 'Honestly, Damon, I'm not concerned about that. It's just so . . . so tacky! I hate lies.'

'You knew there would be a certain amount of subterfuge involved in this venture when you accepted,' he said icily, 'I've apologised for the unforeseen reaction of my uncle. Now I don't want to hear any more about it.'

'Well, there's one other apology I'd appreciate,' Philippa said mutinously. 'It was quite unnecessary to kiss me the . . . the way you did.'

'Just keeping up appearances for the sake of Uncle Richard. Sorry you found it offensive.'

'I did,'

'Don't worry, I won't repeat it.' He glared at her.

'Thank you.' She picked up a magazine, and spent the rest of the journey pretending to read.

It was dark when they arrived in Athens. Like any city airport, it was hectic, and since the Greeks are an exuberant race, the terminal was chaos—excited Greek voices screaming loudly, groups of people embracing, weeping, laughing. Philippa stood beside the luggage carousel, numb and bewildered. Then she saw Damon coming towards her with a little man in tow, who was dressed in a navy blue uniform.

'Philippa, this is Spiro, our chauffeur,' said Damon, turning to the beaming little man—who reminded Philippa of a Kalamati olive, his face was so creased with smiles. Damon said something in rapid Greek. Spiro removed his cap with a sweep, and took a rather battered red carnation from his pocket, which he handed ceremoniously to Philippa. Then he stood back and gazed up at her admiringly.

'Oh, thank you ... Spiro,' she fumbled in the Greek phrase book she had bought the previous week, and tried the phrase 'thank you very much'. This caused Spiro's face to almost split in two with joy, he turned to his employer, and gesticulating wildly, poured forth a torrent of Greek. Damon answered him rather shortly, and indicating the luggage to be stowed in the car, left Spiro to it, while he guided Philippa to the exit.

She sniffed the wilting carnation. 'What a sweet thing to do,' she said. 'What was he saying, Damon?'

'He said you looked like a goddess,' Damon answered crossly.

'How nice of him!'

'I pointed out that you don't have a temper to match.'

'Maybe he thought I looked like a bad-tempered goddess. They weren't always nice, were they?'

'You're right. Goddesses could be quite hard on mere mortals. I think I'll settle for a human woman . . . even if she does object to my kisses.' He installed himself beside her in the car and gave her one of his devastating smiles. Her heart turned over in her breast, and she instantly became all caution.

'I don't object on principle,' she said, trying to control the quiver in her voice, 'but I do think we should stick to the contract as closely as possible, without too much unnecessary play-acting.'

'Ah yes, the contract,' he spat the word out, like an oath. 'By all means, we must be legal.' He hunched his wide shoulders and turned from her to stare moodily out of the window.

Spiro finished stowing the luggage in the trunk and drove them out of the airport, and into Athens, towards the suburb of Hymettus, where Damon had an apartment.

As they climbed the hill to the apartment building, the Acropolis, floodlit against a velvet sky, blazed a welcome. Philippa forgot Damon's pique, forgot that this was the most miserable wedding night in history, for now she was caught in the magic of this most magical of cities. Now she really felt she was in Greece. The graceful lines of the Parthenon, theatrically lit against the dark night, succeeded in driving her doubts into the background. She turned to Damon impulsively.

'Oh, look, look . . . oh, Damon, it's so beautiful!'

Her enthusiasm was infectious. His face cleared. 'After I've collected Athena tomorrow, I'll take you there.'

'Oh, yes! Yes, please!'

'Unfortunately one isn't allowed to walk in the Parthenon now. It's being worn away by all the thousands who walk on it—that, and all the chemicals.'

'Chemicals?'

'Acid rain, and God knows what else, pours over that ancient temple, eroding it slowly, over the years.'

'But that's criminal!' Philippa was indignant. 'Can't anything be done?'

'So far, apart from forbidding pedestrians to keep the pavements from being even more worn away than they are, no one does a thing. Man's greed will finally obliterate one of the most beautiful ruins in the world at this rate. I sit on a committee to try and force the industries to do something about the filth that spews out of their chimneys, but so far we haven't been very effective, I'm afraid.'

'Well, you just keep after them, Damon,' Philippa's amber eyes were alive with concern. 'It's monstrous to think of a beautiful monument like the Parthenon just crumbling away!'

He laughed softly, 'Maybe I'll set you on to them. You look fierce enough to cow them into submission!'

The car drew to a halt at that moment, before a four-storey apartment building of fairly new design. The street was quiet and tree-lined. A gay striped awning shaded the entrance, and next door an elegant taverna sported several red and white umbrellas over small pavement tables, and this looked suitably foreign to Philippa's British eyes.

Damon's apartment occupied the entire top floor of the building, art-deco in design, and decorated in apple green and white, with touches of gold. All the windows had a view of the floodlit Parthenon, which seemed to float in the sky, a sentinel over Athens.

Philippa was introduced to Spiro's wife, Eda, a smiling counterpart to her husband. The couple were the resident staff, apart from a regular daily woman. Eda was overcome to meet her new mistress, and gabbled away in Greek, while showing Philippa over the apartment. And Philippa determined to learn at least a smattering of the language during her stay. The apartment was not overly large. Apart from the servants' quarters, there were two bedrooms, a dining room, and a spacious living room, furnished with green silk sofas and Oriental rugs on highly polished wood floors. Damon had a modest study that seemed to consist of books from floor to ceiling.

After her tour Philippa returned to the living room, where Damon sat, sipping a milky coloured drink. He rose when she came in, and said,

'You must have a glass of ouzo before you go to bed, Pippa.'

'I don't want a drink, thank you. Not after all that champagne.'

'That was hours ago. Besides, Spiro will be very disappointed if you refuse. He put it on ice for us when I phoned him yesterday to say we'd be coming. You can't really say you've arrived in Greece till you've tasted ouzo.' He put some ice in a tall glass and poured some clear liquid over it. As soon as it touched the ice, it became cloudy and gave off a strong scent of aniseed. He topped it up with ice water from a silver jug, and handed it to her. 'There! Your first taste of Greece. Sit here and look at the Acropolis while you drink it—that's appropriate, I think. And sip, don't gulp, it's inclined to be a rough drink.'

'I'm not in the habit of gulping my drinks,' said Philippa. He could be so infuriatingly bossy sometimes, she thought, as she sank into the farthest corner of one of the plump sofas, as far from him as possible.

Damon turned out all the lights, except for one silk-shaded table lamp, and sprawling his massive length in an armchair, lay back with his drink in his hand, staring at the illuminated view in the distance.

Philippa sipped her ouzo. Its coarse aniseed flavour

was refreshing. She sat very still, giving a false air of calm. Here she was, with a man who was legally her husband, but who was virtually a stranger. She was very conscious that she was many miles from home, and another worry was niggling at the corners of her mind. On her tour of the apartment she had only seen two bedrooms, Athena's and the master bedroom. She didn't like to ask Damon about it, since any reference to their contract seemed to enrage him, but she was anxious. And his proximity was overpowering. He had removed the jacket of the navy suit he had worn for the wedding, and put on a short wine silk dressing-gown, and comfy-looking slippers of soft suede. Philippa couldn't take her eyes from those slippers, there was something so intimate about them. They looked so domestic, so . . . married. And Damon was stretched out so lazily, she was more aware than ever of his powerful muscles under the silk robe, of his flat belly and long legs.

She buried her nose in her glass and took a hasty sip of ouzo. It went down the wrong way, and she choked noisily.

'I told you not to gulp,' he said. 'Here!' He poured her a glass of water, then sat at the far end of the sofa. 'Relax, Pippa. When we've finished our drinks we'll turn in, it's been a long day.' There was an agonising silence, during which she was sure he must be able to hear her breathing. Then he continued, 'To put your mind at rest, I'll sleep in my dressing room. There's a bathroom between us, and you can have the key to the door if it makes you feel better.'

'No . . . no, thank you . . . I mean, I don't need a key,' she muttered weakly.

'You plan to push the furniture against the door?' He sounded bitter.

'Certainly not! I mean, I know I can trust you.'

Damon regarded her wearily. 'Some men would

consider that an insult,' he murmured. When she remained silent he continued, with a wry smile, 'Eda and Spiro are most disapproving. I told them you snored!'

Philippa finished her drink. The shadowed room made her feel remote from him, in spite of its hushed intimacy. When she broke the silence her voice sounded strident to her ears.

'Well, I'll go to bed, then. I'm very tired.'

'Goodnight, Pippa.' His gaze never wavered. His eyes were unfathomable, piercing in their intensity.

She rose, and waited for him to give her the light goodnight kiss on the cheek she had come to expect, but he didn't stir.

After an awkward pause she said 'goodnight' once more, and left him sitting in the darkened room, alone.

Lying in the big bed she could see the Acropolis, and, like a dream, the Parthenon seemed to float in the sky. She wondered, briefly, how Martha was faring, on her first night alone, but Martha and London seemed a lifetime away. Philippa felt emptied of all feeling, as if her life had only started when they arrived in this magical city, which sighed, like a promise, in the night.

# CHAPTER SIX

'GOOD morning, *Kyria!*' said Eda in a bright voice. Philippa woke and instantly the events of yesterday flooded back—the wedding, Damon's angry kiss, and her arrival, with her surly groom, to this mysterious city.

Eda flung back the shutters, and the blinding Greek sunlight flooded the apple green room. Sun danced on the walls like music, in a passion of riotous silver. Philippa caught her breath, the light intoxicated her, and the honey-coloured Parthenon, looking more substantial in the morning, beckoned enticingly.

The Greek maid, after a disapproving look at the uncrumpled side of the big bed, set down a silver tray laden with breakfast things. 'You want in bed, or by window, *Kyria?*' she asked.

'Oh, by the window, please,' said Philippa, adding a 'thank you' in wobbly Greek. This released a delighted torrent of liquid-sounding Greek from Eda, not a word of which Philippa recognised. The woman insisted on helping Philippa into her peach robe, and left, still chattering away nineteen to the dozen.

The tray, which was set for two, contained pots of hot coffee and tea, two silver bowls of honey, one creamy and one amber liquid, a heavy cut-crystal dish of yogurt, a bowl of fruit, and, buried in a snowy damask napkin, a loaf of homemade bread, still warm from the oven. There was also iced orange juice in a silver thermos jug.

She poured herself a glass of juice, and was just spreading a slice of fragrant bread with honey, when there was a tap on the door and Damon came into the room. His skin seemed darker than before, and Philippa felt that he had become more exotic-looking since their arrival, as if his Greek heritage became dominant when he breathed the Athenian air. And the thin white silk shirt and dark business suit he wore did nothing to dispel this impression.

'Good morning, Pippa.' His eyes were neon blue in this luminous light, he looked at her tousled blonde hair and filmy negligee with approval. 'You're looking very pretty this morning,' his eyes lingered on the low neck of her peignoir. 'I like your robe.' His frank admiration of her flimsily clad body brought the blood to her face. 'But it won't be as sexy if it's covered with honey,' he teased, when she involuntarily clasped it closer with sticky fingers.

He sat in the chair opposite hers and held out one of the fragile china cups, decorated with a delicate floral design. 'I'll have coffee, please. Black.' Philippa dutifully filled the cup with the strong aromatic brew. 'Thank you. Have you tried the yogurt yet?' Before she had a chance to reply he went on. 'You must. Greek yogurt tastes like cream. It bears no relation to the watery stuff you buy in English shops.'

'I don't like yogurt,' she protested.

'You'll like this.' He put a large spoonful into a bowl and handed it to her. 'Here, try it.' And when she hesitated, irritated once again by his imperiousness, he said sharply, 'Eat it. It's good for you.'

'That's the worst recommendation I know,' she said. 'Things that are "good for you" usually taste awful!' But she tried a spoonful, to avoid an argument, and he was right; it was delicious.

Meanwhile Damon kept babbling—there was no other word for it—never giving her a moment to answer him. What's the matter with him *now*? she wondered, for here was a mood she hadn't encountered before. His eyes kept darting away, then coming back to rest on her with an emotion she couldn't name, but which she found disturbing.

His long, sensitive fingers drummed a tattoo on the table, and his signet ring flashed golden in the sunshine. His restless eyes encountered the double bed.

'That won't do, Pippa,' he said. 'You have to consider my reputation!' She looked at him uncomprehendingly. 'My reputation with the servants!' She still stared. 'The bed, girl, the bed!' he sighed. 'At least try not to advertise the fact that ours is a business arrangement. Rumple both sides, so Eda won't catch on that you sleep all night in splendid isolation.'

He drained his cup and got up. Philippa noticed he hadn't eaten. A slice of bread lay torn to fragments on his plate, beside a half-peeled orange.

'I'm off to get Athena now,' he told her. 'The poor girl will be wild with impatience to come home.'

Athena! The sole reason she was in Greece, and she'd forgotten. Panic swept over Philippa. What if Athena didn't like her? What if she didn't like Athena!

'How ... how long will you be?' she faltered, praying she would have time to regain her composure.

'About an hour.' He stopped for a moment on his way out. 'And, Pippa?'

'Yes.'

'Don't look so worried. Athena's a nice child—far nicer than your spoilt little sister!' His door slammed punctuated this parting shot.

In an hour's time Philippa was dressed, and waiting for them. She looked calm enough, in a softly tailored pant-suit, her honey-coloured hair caught loosely at her neck with a jade barette. But her fingers twisted together nervously as she stood in the comfortable living room, and when she heard Damon's voice in the outer hall, her heartbeat quickened painfully.

Then he was in the room, his arm around the shoulders of a small, dark-eyed teenager, who looked suspiciously at Philippa during the introductions.

Athena was small and slender, and as unlike Damon as possible. Her face was very pale, and her short hair was blue-black and straight.

'How do you do?' she said stiffly. Her English was practically flawless.

'Rather nervous at the moment, Athena,' Philippa grinned, 'and I suspect you are too.'

There was no answering smile from the hostile Athena. Instead, she pointedly turned to Damon and started speaking in Greek, clutching at his sleeve possessively.

'Now, Kookla,' he gently loosened her fingers, 'we must talk in English when Pippa's with us. She doesn't understand Greek.'

'But I mean to learn,' Philippa assured him. 'Will you help me, Athena? I'd learn so much faster if you would.'

'I do not think I would be a very good teacher for you,' Athena answered coldly. 'Perhaps Uncle Damon can hire someone to teach you.'

'If you want all those new clothes for Crete, perhaps I should hire *you*!' Damon teased his niece, then explained to Philippa, 'Athena was asking me for an advance on her allowance. She's seen some clothes that she can't live without—eh, Kookla?' He smiled at his niece tenderly. It was clear that he loved her dearly. It was also clear, from the smouldering resentment she bore his new wife, that Athena adored her uncle. Philippa sighed. Winning Athena's affection was not going to be easy.

'I've ordered some coffee for us,' she said, 'and you, Athena, have you had breakfast?'

'Thank you, I breakfasted hours ago,' she contrived to make it sound like a reproof, 'and I do not wish any coffee. I will go and change now, out of *this*.' She indicated the school uniform she was wearing.

'Well, don't be long, Athena,' said Damon. 'I want to take you and Pippa to visit the Acropolis, and I have a business meeting at two.'

The child threw a glance of distaste at Philippa before replying, 'Perhaps you would prefer to go alone with your wife.'

'Oh, Athena, please come too,' Philippa answered hastily, trying desperately to establish some warmth between them.

'I have seen the Acropolis before,' was the crushing reply. Philippa noticed a look of displeasure on Damon's handsome face.

'But *I* haven't,' she said, before he had a chance to say anything. 'And it would be so nice for me to have a woman around . . . to share my first impressions.'

Athena's set face softened slightly. No fourteen-year-old dislikes being called a woman. 'Very well, I shall come. If Uncle Damon wishes it,' she amended.

'I do,' said Damon, and then added something sharply in Greek, which made Athena's pale little face turn scarlet. With a stifled sob she ran from the room, nearly knocking over Eda, who came in at that moment with the coffee tray.

After Eda had left them a black silence filled the sunny room. Damon's curved lower lip jutted out in a way Philippa was beginning to recognise as a danger signal.

She shifted the silver coffee pot into a more convenient position on the tray.

'Coffee, Damon?'

'Yes—black.'

She handed him his steaming cup.

'To match your mood?' she asked mildly.

He turned on her the full force of his smouldering blue eyes. 'If I'm in a mood, as you call it, it's with reason. I will not tolerate rudeness. Athena was rude and I told her so. It won't happen again.'

Philippa stirred sugar thoughtfully into her coffee. 'You surprise me, Damon,' she said.

He raised an enquiring eyebrow. 'May I ask why?'

'I always thought of you as a realist. It seems I was wrong.'

'Indeed?'

'Look, Damon,' she put aside her coffee and leaned towards him, her tawny eyes looking full into his angry blue ones, 'it's not my business how you treat your niece, but if you want her to like me you're going about it the wrong way.'

'Indeed?' he repeated.

'It's perfectly normal for her to resent me, particularly since it's apparent she's dotty over you. Reading her the riot act isn't going to make her like me any better. I'm surprised you can't see that.'

'You know nothing about me,' he said frostily, 'how can you know what I expect . . . from anyone?'

'Well, don't expect too much from her. Give me time to win her. I can't do that if you keep barking at her because she doesn't jump for joy every time she's around me.'

'I hope you're not going to suggest I'm as submissive with Athena as you are with Martha!'

Philippa flushed with temper, but she held it in check. 'I'm simply telling you that you're making it impossible for me to do the job I was hired for. At this rate I might as well quit before I start.'

'Very well,' he conceded with bad grace, 'I'll let you handle it. But I warn you, Philippa, I won't allow you to knuckle under to a series of adolescent insults— even if that's what you're used to at home.'

Athena came back at this moment, which prevented Philippa making an angry reply. The girl had changed into a skirt and light sweater. She looked younger, and seemed more vulnerable than when she was wearing her severe school uniform. She held herself very upright, and oozed jealousy from every pore. Philippa felt a wave of sympathy for the child, and smiled warmly at her, but the young girl's face remained stony, and it was in an atmosphere crackling with tension that they left for their sightseeing expedition.

Spiro drove them to the *plaka*, or market place, at the foot of the Acropolis. Damon gave him instructions to return for the two girls later that afternoon, then silently led the way. They started to climb one of the narrow streets which wound up towards the unblinking splendour of the Parthenon. Small tavernas and bars dotted the pavement with tables. Vines, trained to creep over trellises, would give shade to hot and weary customers in the summer. The scent of herbs mingled with the smell of coffee. Black-clad women, dark scarves tied over their hair, hurried by, crossing themselves when they passed one of the countless churches. The window of a *kafeinion* displayed freshly baked pastries, bursting with honey and nuts. Jewellery stores glittered. Kiosks offered gaudy worry beads and postcards for the tourists who would throng these streets in summer. Now, apart from a few Germans and Japanese, hung about with their inevitable cameras, the place was relatively empty.

They left the *plaka* behind and started climbing the hill which led to the Parthenon, crown of the Acropolis. When they reached the restraining railing Damon made a space for her in the sparse crowd, so she would have a clear view. Philippa was tall enough to see without difficulty over the railing, and she gazed in awe at the regal and majestic Parthenon, its graceful, fluted pillars gleaming golden in the sunshine.

She turned to look at the Erectheum, its slender caryatids, or maidens, timeless as Athena herself, looking far more serene than the goddess's glowering namesake sulking beside her. The pathway Philippa stood on undulated like a sea, it was so worn by the countless feet that had trodden there. Her breath caught in her throat. It's real, she thought, it's not a dream. I'm really in Greece, seeing all this with my own eyes. I don't have to pinch myself to see if I'm dreaming. It's real!

She stole a look at Damon and was startled to see his eyes were bright with tears. She could understand that. It was so wonderful here, so moving. She longed to touch him, let him know she understood. But she didn't dare.

He sensed her eyes upon him and turned away. 'Well, that's the famous Parthenon,' he said gruffly, 'just a heap of crumbling stones.'

'It's one of the most beautiful things I've ever seen,' she said, 'and although it's a ruin, it's still unbelievably alive, and it always will be.' Now she did find the courage to lay her slim hand lightly on his sleeve. 'How proud you must be to have Greek blood in your veins, Damon—to be a part of all this.'

His face lost its mask of sadness. 'You have quite a heritage yourself, Pippa,' he said. 'England isn't exactly a new country.'

'But you have a foot in both places.' She turned to the silent Athena. 'You both do. I think Athens is wonderful,' she went on impulsively. 'I wish I had roots here.'

'You do,' Athena said. 'You have married someone who is partly Greek, which makes you partly Greek too. You are part of our family, whether we like it or not,' she added, just loud enough for Philippa to hear, then she caught her eye and had the grace to blush, kicking the dusty path with her sandalled foot.

'What's the matter with you *now*, Athena?' demanded Damon, sounding dangerously irritable.

'Nothing, Uncle Damon,' Athena replied, close to tears.

'I think it's time for lunch, Damon,' Philippa said diplomatically. 'I don't know about you two, but historic sights make me very hungry!'

Glancing at the gold Piaget watch strapped to his lean wrist, Damon agreed. Particularly if he wanted to get to his meeting in time, he said.

'I thought everything closed for the afternoon in Greece,' said Philippa. 'Isn't there a siesta hour?'

'That's where the British part of me takes over,' explained Damon, guiding them towards a small taverna at the foot of the hill. 'I don't usually take siestas. And certainly not until it gets hot. My Greek associates deplore this, but I get a lot of work done.' Holding Philippa firmly by the arm, he helped her down the path. The incline of the hill forced her to lean against him, and she was physically aware of his lithe muscular body pressed close to her side. She tried to get more control of her sliding feet, to stand without his aid, but he set such a brisk pace she was unable to pull away. Athena lagged behind, and the two adults were seated at a small table outside the café by the time she joined them.

Damon ordered for them, a simple lunch of omelettes filled with salty *feta* cheese, a plate of tomatoes and black olives, and slices of crusty Greek bread, beige in colour rather than white. They drank chilled retsina, which Damon assured her came fresh from the blue cans of the *plaka*, and wasn't the bottled kind. At first she wasn't sure about retsina, but after her first sip she decided she liked its resiny flavour. Athena drank orange soda, and remained silent.

The sun was warmer now, so Philippa removed her green linen jacket and rolled up the sleeves of her pink silk shirt. She looked at Damon sitting across from her, his blue eyes squinting against the dazzle. He's quite the handsomest man here, she thought, and felt unaccountably proud that she wore his wedding ring, even if it wasn't quite the way it appeared to be.

After a leisurely lunch Damon got up to leave them.

'Stay a little longer and enjoy a baklava,' he said. He turned to Athena. 'Your new aunt has a sweet tooth, and I intended to indulge it.'

'She will get fat,' said the girl, finally breaking her silence.

'Not Pippa. She's not the type.' He turned his attention to Philippa. 'We're dining out tonight with some business associates—a very dressy affair. Now, reluctantly I must leave you both. Athena, be a good girl now!' He planted a kiss on his niece's cloudy face, and after a fraction of a second, kissed Philippa quickly, full on her mouth. His lips were warm, and she fought the desire to put her arms around him and prolong the delicious pleasure his kiss gave her.

When she had collected herself, and Damon's long-legged figure had disappeared in the maze of streets, the waiter brought them their paklavas—layers of *filo* pastry, thin as tissue paper, stuffed with walnuts and drenched with honey. She savoured every sweet, delicious bite, then she turned to her sullen companion.

'What shall we do till Spiro comes for us, Athena? Do you have any plans?'

'My uncle has told me I am to entertain you this afternoon.'

'Poor you! That sounds dreadful,' Philippa commiserated. 'What would you do if I wasn't around?' The girl merely lifted her shoulders in an elaborate shrug. 'Well, since you don't have any ideas, I'd like to continue sightseeing.' She wasn't going to pander to Athena's mood. 'Isn't there a museum on the Acropolis?'

'A small one, yes. And some caves in the hillside,

where local children sometimes play and look for shards.'

'I don't think I'll look for shards today. I'm scared of caves. I suffer from claustrophobia,' Philippa explained.

'I do not know that word. What does it mean?'

'That I panic if I'm in a small space without light.'

'The museum is small. But there is light.'

'Then let's look at it, shall we?' She smiled tentatively, but got no response.

They started to walk across the paved courtyard, towards the museum which was at the far side. Suddenly Athena spoke.

'How did you meet Uncle Damon?' she demanded, stopping in the centre of the pathway.

'I worked for him.' They stood facing each other on the narrow track.

'As his secretary?'

'No. I cooked for him.'

Athena's childish mouth opened in amazement. 'You were his *cook*?' she exclaimed.

'Not full time,' Philippa smiled. 'I run . . . ran . . . my own catering business. Do you know what that is, Athena? It means preparing food for dinner parties, cocktail parties, things like that.'

'You were his *servant*? Like . . . like Eda?' The girl's voice was filled with contempt.

'Yes, I suppose I was,' Philippa looked unwaveringly into Athena's belligerent eyes. 'Does it shock you?'

'I did not think my uncle would choose to marry a *servant*,' Athena said scornfully.

Philippa gave a light laugh, 'Why, Athena, I do believe you're a snob!' she teased. The girl didn't reply, but turning on her heel continued climbing. Philippa followed, racking her brains to think of something that would break this impasse. Athena stopped beside a hollowed-out room carved into the hillside. It had a crudely constructed door at the opening. This was propped open, showing a makeshift trestle table, covered with shards of pottery.

'This is perhaps interesting to you,' Athena volunteered, 'they have started another dig in this area. These are the pieces of pottery they have found. It is allowed to go in and examine them,' she continued when Philippa hesitated. Since this was the first time Athena had been even remotely friendly, Philippa, much against her instinct, walked into the dark room and looked at the shards. They were labelled and sorted into various heaps. She leaned over one pile that had a design on the fragments.

'This looks interesting, Athena,' she said. 'I wonder if they'll be able to construct a vase or amphora from these?' But there was no reply. She turned around, just in time to see Athena straining to push the heavy door shut. Philippa raced towards the rapidly closing door, but she was too late. It closed with a sickening thud and she was alone in the pitch black room.

'Athena . . . no!' she screamed. Then she stood still, shaking with terror. She couldn't see a thing. The dark felt like a blanket, suffocating her. She stretched her arms above her head, and easily touched the low ceiling. Taking a step backwards, she bumped into the table, and a fragment of pottery fell to the dirt floor. Easing her way slowly along the edge of the trestle, she found the wall and followed it, inch by inch, until her fingers encountered the wooden door. In relief she felt for the handle. But the door was uniformly even. There was no handle inside, and not a chink of light came through. Panic swept over her again and she pushed against the door with all her strength, pounding the rough wood with ineffectual fists.

'Athena . . . help . . . somebody *help me*!' she yelled as loudly as she could. The room echoed her cries mockingly. Sliding to the floor, she wondered for a moment if she would faint, so great was her terror. Her breath was coming in painful gulps, and tears of frustration slid down her cheeks. With an immense effort she controlled herself.

She realised there was no use hammering on the door and screaming. There were no people around this time of day, and even if there had been it was unlikely they could have heard her. But since this was used as a store room, someone would be coming here eventually. It was just a case of . . . how long?

She felt something crawling on her ankle, and jerked away in disgust. Trying to control her panic, she deliberately took several deep breaths and started talking aloud. Her voice sounded muffled in the stifling darkness.

'Please, God, send somebody soon. Please, dear God, don't leave me here too long. Please send Damon. Oh, Damon! Darling Damon, please help me! Please, God, send Damon,' she sobbed, and through her panic she was aware that, more than anyone else in the world, she wanted Damon. Only he could comfort her. In his arms alone would she feel safe.

Her tears subsided, and she huddled on the floor of the cave-like room, hugging her knees, allowing her thoughts to dwell, unchecked, on Damon, pretending that his arms cradled her, his hands caressing, comforting. She lost track of the time, sitting with the blackness pressing against her like a wall, only the thought of Damon keeping her from total hysteria.

Then she heard a muffled scuffling outside, and with a creak the heavy door was pushed aside. A narrow shaft of blinding sunshine cut through the darkness like a dagger. For a moment, so powerful was her need of him, she thought it was Damon silhouetted in the narrow doorway. Instead, Spiro came towards her, closely followed by an ashen Athena.

Stiffly Philippa got to her feet. She realised she must look a wreck. Her pant-suit was stained with mud, her face streaked with tears.

'*Kyria!*' Spiro put out his hand to assist his young mistress. She took a shuddering gulp of fresh air, and became so dizzy she had to cling to his arm to prevent herself from falling.

'Are you all right, Philippa?' Athena's lips were bloodless.

'I think so.' Assisted by Spiro, Philippa slowly made her way to the waiting car.

Philippa looked at Athena. 'How long was I in ... in that place?' She asked.

'About an hour. I tried to open the door, but it was too heavy for me, so I phoned Spiro to come.'

'You didn't seem to have any trouble closing it,' Philippa said bitterly, knowing Spiro couldn't understand them.

'There is a groove. The door falls into it once it is closed. I could not lift it.' Athena lifted her eyes, which were swimming with tears. 'I did try to open it, Philippa—I swear it!'

'Well, thanks for getting Spiro,' said Philippa. 'I don't think I would have stayed sane much longer.' She was aware of being tired to the point of exhaustion.

The blessed daylight was making her eyes smart ... not that she cared, she was so happy to be freed from that dark prison ... gratefully she leaned back against the leather car seat, blinking in the sunshine, allowing her limbs to relax on the silent drive back to Hymettus.

She knew Athena was anxiously waiting for her to discuss the incident, to be forgiven. But she was too weary to talk. She would deal with Athena, and all the problems attached to that young lady, later. Now all she could think of was a long hot bath, a strong cup of tea, and a serious re-examination of her feelings for her employer-husband, Damon Everett.

# CHAPTER SEVEN

AFTER a strong cup of tea, which she made herself since it seemed beyond Eda's comprehension that anyone would want tea when coffee was available, Philippa took a leisurely bath in the master bedroom's sunken travertine tub. This gave her time to think. She needed time to sort out her feelings, and face a fact she knew she had been avoiding for some days.

Lying in the scented water, her tall well-formed body relaxed at last, she thought back on the afternoon's ordeal. It was time to be honest with herself. Only the thought of Damon's strong arms, the fantasy that he loved her, had kept her from a total breakdown.

She could no longer hide from herself that she had fallen in love with him—deeply, irrevocably in love. She knew that a love of this intensity was possible only once in a lifetime. She also knew that she mustn't give herself away. While she was with him she must constantly watch herself, so that he would never guess how deeply she cared. Because it was plain he didn't feel the same way. From the beginning he had stressed the businesslike nature of their relationship . . . 'The last thing I want is an emotional entanglement' . . . Well, she must make sure he never found out. She would be constantly on her guard, and somehow she would carry the sweet pain of loving him, and not tell a soul.

She climbed out of the cooling water and dried herself on one of the thick peach-coloured bath towels. Then she dropped the towel and looked at herself in the steamy, mirror-covered wall. I wish I wasn't so tall, she thought wistfully, for the umpteenth time since her adolescence. But she wasn't blind, she could see that she had high, firm breasts, a slender waist, and sensuously rounded hips. She was aware that when she held herself proudly, and did not hide her attractiveness in dowdy clothes, she looked good. If Damon could see me like this, she wondered, naked and unashamed, would he still want no part of an emotional entanglement? She flushed hotly at this illicit thought, and bundling herself in a terry robe went to the bedroom to repair her damaged nails.

She dressed with care for the evening's party, piling her hair high on her head the way she had been shown. She wore the wine silk dress, with the pearls Damon had given her for the wedding. They seemed to draw their creamy lustre from her satiny skin, so that she glowed in the warm scented gown like a pearl herself.

When she went into the living room Damon was already there. Athena, who was not invited to the party, was sitting in the shadows, a pale little ghost.

Damon, in the act of pouring a glass of ouzo, turned and stared at his wife. 'That's a very good colour for you,' he said at last, offering her the drink, but she refused it. Her nerves were still raw from the afternoon's adventure, and God knew what emotions alcohol might release. 'Now what's all this Spiro tells me about you getting yourself locked up this afternoon?'

Athena gave her an agonised look, then stared miserably at the floor.

'I was very stupid, Damon,' Philippa said, as lightly as she could. 'I started poking around in that storeroom near the dig ... the one on the Acropolis ... and the door swung shut on me. Athena couldn't open it, so she got Spiro. I wasted the afternoon, and I didn't even get a good look at the shards, it was too dark,' she forced a giggle.

'For God's sake be more careful, Pippa,' he said roughly. 'That place is strictly out of bounds. Didn't Athena tell you?'

'Oh, she said something, but you know me—I don't always listen,' Philippa replied, before Athena could say a word.

'Well, I advise you to listen in future.' He sounded irritated, but perhaps this was better than sympathy. Sympathy from Damon now might have released another flood of tears. 'If Athena hadn't been there you might have been trapped all night.'

Philippa repressed a shudder. 'I know. Shouldn't you change, Damon?' she asked, anxious to change the subject, 'We only have half an hour.'

He gave her a long hard look, then abruptly handed her a large jewel box that had been lying on the chair beside him, there was a key in the lock.

'These are for you,' he said shortly. 'I'll put them in the bedroom safe, you can examine the contents tomorrow. But first let me choose something to go with your dress.' He opened the lid, poked around in the box, and bringing out a pair of ruby and pearl ear-rings and a heavy ruby and pearl bracelet, said, 'Here, these should do. They match that silk well.' He thrust them into her unresisting hands and left the room.

Philippa looked at the exquisite jewellery lying heavy in her hand. The rubies shone like blood. She stood in front of the mantel mirror and put on the ear-rings, standing back to admire the effect of the glowing stones against her creamy neck. There was a broken sob from the direction of Athena's armchair. Philippa took a handkerchief from her evening purse and handed it to the girl.

'Here, mop up.'

Athena gulped miserably and dabbed her eyes. 'I feel so awful, Philippa. I behaved so badly.'

'Yes, you did. But it's over now. Now you must forget it.'

'How can I forget it,' Athena wailed, 'when you've been so kind? I was sure you would tell Uncle Damon about me, but you didn't. Instead you protected me. Can you ever forgive me?'

Philippa perched herself on the edge of the chair and put her arm round the child's shaking shoulders. 'I've forgiven you already, darling,' she forced the girl to look into her eyes, 'and I want to be your friend. Will you be mine?'

In a passion of tears Athena buried her face in Philippa's breast. 'Yes! Oh yes! And Pippa . . . can I call you Pippa like Uncle Damon does? . . . I did try to let you out. The minute I pushed the door shut I was sorry . . . but then I couldn't move the door. I did try. You do believe me?' Her tear-stained face was filled with entreaty.

'I believe you, Athena. Now you must stop crying or your Uncle Damon will smell a rat,' Athena looked mystified. 'Will get suspicious,' Philippa explained. 'Also you're making the front of my dress damp.' Athena gave her a watery smile. 'Now, could you help me with this bracelet? I can't seem to work the clasp.'

And that was how Damon found them—Philippa on her knees holding out her arm to Athena, who bent lower when Damon came in to hide her tear-swollen eyes.

Damon drove the car to the party. On the way he slowed down and turning to Philippa said, 'I'm perfectly aware, Pippa, that something happened between you and Athena this afternoon. I suppose it's useless to ask you to tell me about it?' He again turned his attention to the winding road.

'Absolutely useless,' she agreed. She kept her eyes

on his stern profile, the cleft in his chin accentuated by the faint glow from the dashboard. His beautifully shaped hands lay lightly on the steering wheel.

'I shall find out eventually.' He was as smooth as silk. 'At least the child seems better behaved than this morning. I congratulate you on your victory.' He glanced at her again, and gave her a smile that made her heart turn over in her breast. Hastily she looked away. The need to touch him was so acute it was a fierce pain. To protect herself she answered curtly,

'Congratulations aren't necessary, Damon. It's what you're paying me for, isn't it?' She saw his mouth tighten, his beautiful mouth that she longed to kiss. But he remained silent, and she turned to the window and studied the passing scenery intently.

Nothing more was said for the rest of the drive. Mr and Mrs Damon Everett, each wrapped in their secret thoughts, rode through the brilliant Athenian streets, the silence between them lying like a double-edged sword.

The dinner party was an elegant affair for twenty guests. Philippa was aware that she looked as well groomed as the other women, and she was pleasantly conscious of the discreet admiration in the dark eyes of the men when they were introduced to the new Mrs Everett.

It was the custom, she discovered, for the males and females to separate at such gatherings, the men presumably to discuss business, their wives to gossip about children and household affairs. Philippa found this old-fashioned and tedious, and resolved to try and prevent it happening at any parties she would be giving.

However, her hostess spoke quite good English, and the other women, using her as interpreter, asked so many questions about England and her life there . . . 'Have you ever met the Queen? Do you chase foxes?'

. . . that the segregation policy of Grecian entertaining was soon forgotten.

At dinner she was seated between her host and a grey-haired gentleman who also spoke English, and whose frank approval of her was flattering, and an unusual situation for Philippa, who was used to Martha being the centre of male attention.

The dinner was very good, and a number of the dishes were new to her. She decided to start collecting Greek recipes to use when she got back to England and started working again. She mustn't let herself forget that reality, no matter how much she might be lulled into feeling this new life with Damon was for ever. She glanced across the candlelit table at him. He was leaning towards his right-hand companion, a sophisticated brunette, sleek as polished ebony. Damon and this woman, whose name she couldn't remember from the flurry of introductions, but who, judging from the warmth of her greeting, had known Damon for some time, were deep in intimate conversation. Her dark eyes never left his face. Then she said something in a low voice and lightly touched his wrist. He tilted his head back and laughed appreciatively, then raised his glass in a private toast to the dark-eyed beauty. He was obviously having a lovely time. A stab of jealousy cut through Philippa like a knife. At that moment he caught her eye, his brows raised quizzically, and she hastily turned her attention back to her grey-haired dinner partner.

After dinner, when the men were left to enjoy their brandy, Philippa tried to approach Damon's lovely table companion, but discovered she did not speak any English. The two women eyed each other curiously, and Philippa wondered if she imagined hostility in the other woman's gaze.

Damon seemed in splendid spirits on the drive home. He turned the car radio on and hummed along with the Greek bouzouki music, sometimes singing a snatch of the words.

'You're very silent, Pippa,' he observed between songs. 'Didn't you enjoy the party?'

'Yes. I'm not sure about the segregation of the sexes, though. That seems a bit archaic.'

His eloquent brows arched into their characteristic question mark. 'Segregation?'

'Before dinner. All the men herded together in one end of the room, and we poor women left to fend for ourselves and talk about . . . about babies, I suppose.' She was feeling unaccountably cross with him.

'So *that's* what you talk about!' His mouth curled in amusement. 'I didn't know you were interested in that sort of thing Pippa?'

'I'm not . . . I mean . . . I like children, of course . . . that's not what I mean at all, Damon.'

'No?' She was silent. 'What *do* you mean, then?'

'Nothing. Forget it.' The music filled the leather-scented interior of the car. They started to climb towards the city. It was Philippa who spoke first now. 'The dinner was very good. I must start taking notes for recipes I want to try.'

'You miss cooking already?'

'I don't *miss* it exactly. But I need some authentic Greek dishes to offer my clients when I get . . . when I get home.'

'Ah—Philippa's Catering. Your business, of course.' He switched the radio off.

After a few minutes she asked, 'Did you enjoy the dinner, Damon?'

'I enjoyed the whole evening. Although I must agree with you that we have a dreadful habit of separating men and women at parties in this country.'

'At least we get to eat together,' said Philippa. 'I mean, it was nice to talk to . . . Mr Caravias? . . . Am I pronouncing his name right?'

'Quite right. You have a nice accent, Pippa. I'm delighted you think it worth your while to try to learn a little of the language during your short stay.' That hurt her as much as his flirtation with the dark beauty.

'I missed a lot of names, though,' she told him. 'There seemed to be so many people. The name of that gorgeous woman you were sitting next to at dinner, for instance. I didn't catch her name.'

'Which particular gorgeous woman do you mean, Pippa? I was seated between two.' There was laughter in his voice, and she could cheerfully have strangled him.

'Damon, honestly! You know the one I mean. You were talking to her exclusively through dinner. You didn't say a word to anyone else!' She was horrified at the aggrieved note that had crept into her voice. It didn't seem to upset Damon however, he sounded positively gleeful.

'Oh, you mean Thalia,' he replied, 'Thalia Speroudakis. I've known her for years. She *is* gorgeous, isn't she?' he added unnecessarily.

Philippa agreed, gloomily, that she was. Then she said, 'Is it *Miss* Speroudakis?'

'No. She was married.'

'*Was?*'

'She's recently widowed.'

'She seemed very merry, if you don't mind me saying so.'

'I don't mind at all, Pippa,' she could have sworn he repressed a chuckle, 'there's no reason for her to be otherwise. Her husband was much older. And while they respected each other, I know it wasn't a love match.'

'How do you know that?'

'Thalia confided in me. We're very close friends.' He turned on the radio again and so terminated the conversation.

Philippa's thoughts were in turmoil. Was Damon telling her, in his own oblique way, that he was in love with this Thalia Speroudakis? And if he *was* in love with her why hadn't he asked *her* to marry him, rather than Philippa? Perhaps, she reasoned, perhaps he hadn't known she was widowed. Maybe her husband had only recently died, and tonight was the first time Damon discovered Thalia was free. If so he was being remarkably cheerful about it, considering he was married himself. But of course he wasn't really married, and he would have explained that to Thalia during dinner—told her to be patient until he could rid himself of this redundant, fake wife, and tomorrow he would ask Philippa to release him before the contract expired. Pay her off, and that would be that.

But of course he couldn't do that, they'd only been married a couple of days! How would it look if he dumped his bride so quickly for another? No, most likely he had explained the situation to Thalia, and she had promised to wait. She certainly hadn't seemed downcast, flirting with Damon so shamelessly. This time next year she and Damon will be living 'happily ever after', Philippa thought, and Athens and Crete will be just a memory for me. The prospect did not please, and so it was a very subdued Philippa who meekly said goodnight after his customary peck on the cheek. And in her lonely bed the image of Damon and Thalia continued to haunt her dreams.

The following morning she was awakened by Athena bearing the breakfast tray. It was again set for two, but it was soon apparent that Philippa's breakfast companion this morning was not to be Damon, but his niece. Athena perched herself on the bed and poured orange juice for both of them. This morning she was very different from the sullen girl of yesterday. She fairly bubbled with enthusiasm, and asked questions a mile a minute. She noticed the framed photograph of

Martha on the bedside table and was immediately all
curiosity. Philippa told her it was of her younger
sister.

'You have a sister, Pippa?' Athena said. 'You are so
lucky! I always longed for a sister—and brothers too.
But soon I shall have some little cousins to love, won't
I?'

'Wha-what do you mean?' asked the bewildered
Philippa.

'Why, when you and Uncle Damon have babies.
They will be like sisters and brothers to me. Oh,
Pippa, won't it be lovely?' She bounced up and down
with pleasure. 'Can't you just picture them? Little
girls, blonde like you. And dear little dark-haired boys
with blue eyes,' Philippa was dumb with embarrassment. 'Why Pippa, you're *blushing*! You must not
be shy. I am quite grown-up. I know where babies
come from,' Athena giggled.

'I'm sure you do,' said Philippa, attempting
nonchalance, 'but I . . . that is . . . we don't necessarily
plan to have . . . a family. I mean, it doesn't follow that
because one's married one will automatically have
children . . .' She was interrupted by Athena's laughter.

'Do not worry about *that*, Pippa! The men in our
family have always been very virile. Of course you and
Uncle Damon will have children. You just see!'

'Yes . . . well, at the moment I'm still on my
honeymoon Athena,' Philippa smiled feebly, willing
Athena to shut up. 'I think it's a bit early to be
thinking of babies while I'm still a bride.'

'Of course it is early, Pippa,' Athena agreed, 'but
this time next year?' She gave a knowing look and
mercifully changed the subject. 'Now hurry and get
dressed. I want to take you to the museum, and then
to eat *galaktobouriko*.'

Philippa dressed hurriedly, half hoping Damon

would knock on her door to say good morning. But when she joined Athena, who was waiting impatiently with Spiro, she learned he had left hours before, and, although she knew it was irrational, she was hurt.

Later, when the two girls had walked their feet off exploring the ground floor of the splendid Athens museum, and Philippa had fallen in love with the bronze Poseidon (he reminded her slightly of Damon), and marvelled that the statue of the god of the sea had indeed been found *in* the sea near the cape of Artemision, they went to one of the elegant restaurants in the main square. Seated at an outdoor table, they ate *galaktobouriko*, which turned out to be *filo* pastry filled with custard and drizzled with thick amber syrup, so that even Philippa's sweet tooth was satiated. She sat, dazed with a surfeit of sugar, while the cacophony of the Athenian traffic, which seemed either hurtling along at breakneck speed, or jammed to a halt, swirled around her.

'Did you enjoy the *galaktobourika*, Pippa?' Athena's voice broke in.

'Mmmm, it was as good as anything I've eaten since I arrived in Greece.' This was true.

'As good as the food at the party last night?'

Philippa realised she couldn't remember much about the food last night. Her attention had been focused on Damon and Thalia. She could have been eating sawdust for all she remembered. 'Quite as good,' she agreed.

'Didn't you enjoy the party?'

Not wanting to give herself away, Philippa answered hastily, 'Of course. It was ... more formal ... than parties in England. But I had a good time. And Damon had a chance to talk to an old friend of his, a very beautiful lady called Thalia Speroudakis. Do you know her, Athena?' she asked offhandedly.

'Yes, I know her very well. She was a friend of my mother's.'

'She and Damon seemed to have a lot to talk over. I guess they haven't met for a long time?' Philippa prayed she wasn't being obvious, but she had to find out all she could, even if it hurt her.

'My mother once thought Uncle Damon and Madame Speroudakis might marry. But he always had so many ladies, we could never tell if he was serious or not.' This was an unsettling piece of information.

With elaborate casualness Philippa said, 'It's funny, somehow I can't see Damon as a ladies' man.'

'The ladies always seemed to be pursuing *him*. My mother used to tease him about it.'

'Madame Speroudakis . . . did she pursue him?'

'More than any of the others. But she could not catch him,' Athena gave a giggle.

Not *yet*, she hasn't! Philippa thought grimly, but judging from last night she hasn't given up hope. 'She's certainly a very lovely woman,' she said, rubbing salt into the wound.

'Not as lovely as you, Pippa,' Athena replied loyally. 'You are so blonde and tall—like one of the caryatids on the Erectheum on our Acropolis.'

'Supporting a roof on my head? That explains why I have a headache,' sighed Philippa. For indeed the combination of sugar, sunshine, and repressed jealousy had produced a slight headache.

Athena was all sympathy and insisted on returning home at once so that Philippa could rest. Once in her room, Philippa dutifully swallowed the aspirins that were offered, and lay on her bed to recover before getting ready for a reception she was to attend with Damon.

She turned over the snippets of information she had learned. The image of Damon as a rake was quite a revelation. Surely, she thought, if he had so many women in his life he could have asked one of them to act as married chaperone. It sounded as if they were all anxious to trap him; the idea of a summer as Mrs Everett would have appealed to any number of his conquests. And no doubt he wouldn't have had to confine himself to a marriage in name only, not with a lady like Thalia; she appeared only too eager to jump into bed with him, Philippa thought nastily. But of course that very eagerness might be a mark against them. For how could he rely on them quietly going out of his life at the end of the appointed time? With a woman like Philippa, a woman he was not attracted to, one he could treat solely as an employee he was quite safe. He believed she felt nothing for him, and therefore was no threat to his precious freedom.

Little did he guess that she burned with jealousy every time she even thought about him with any of his wretched females. He could not know that she *ached* to have him touch her, caress her, to release the torrent of passion locked within her. That to be his, body and soul, was becoming an obsession, so that his physical presence was both ardently desired and dreaded by her, it was so exquisitely painful.

Her headache had subsided now, but the pain in her heart hadn't. It remained, a sad little stone lying in her breast.

# CHAPTER EIGHT

Two days later they left for Crete. In spite of the help of Eda and Spiro who took care of the packing and bought the first class tickets on the ferry, there was still a lot to do. Athena needed clothes for Chania, and Philippa needed sunglasses and sun-tan lotion, for Crete is the farthest south of all the Greek islands, and while it was still cool in Athens, the sun would already be baking the rocky cliffs and windswept valleys there.

After they had bought Athena's new things Philippa prowled around the smart shops on her own for a couple of hours. She discovered that Damon had deposited a staggering amount of spending money in her account, and felt free to be extravagant. She purchased a narrow gold chain with a charm representing an ancient Grecian coin, and a gold ring set with amethysts. These were for Martha. Later Philippa sat at one of the outdoor restaurants sipping lemonade, while she wrote a four-page letter to her sister trying to describe Athens and her life, without giving anything away. She found it increasingly difficult to live on several levels of play-acting. So far her correspondence with Martha had consisted of postcards, and she decided to try and keep it that way as much as possible. There was a limit to how much information could be put on a postcard.

Their last evening in Athens Damon took Philippa and Athena to dinner at Phaleron Harbour. It was Athena's favourite place, and as soon as they arrived Philippa could understand why. To the left lay the harbour, the water black as silk. Right by the water's edge were the restaurant tables under canvas awnings,

lights strung haphazardly over them. When they
caught the breeze they would cast a momentary
diamond glitter on to the inky water. The restaurants
themselves were on the other side of the road, and the
waiters, trays piled high with food, would thread their
way perilously through the traffic to serve the diners.

They found an empty table, and after ordering ate
the good Greek bread which had come to the table in a
silver-gilt basket, washing it down with glasses of rich,
sweet Mavrodaphne.

Athena was delighted that Philippa approved her
taste in dining out. 'I knew you would like it here,
Pippa,' she said, 'you are not stuck-up like so many of
Uncle Damon's other ladies were.'

'Don't be silly, Kookla,' Damon broke in. 'I've
never known any stuck-up ladies!'

'You *have*,' Athena insisted. 'When we came here
with Madame Speroudakis she did not like it one bit.
She said it was common,' she confided to Philippa.

'Madame Speroudakis was wearing a long dress and
it rained that night,' Damon pointed out. 'Pippa, very
sensibly, is wearing a short dress, and the weather's
perfect.'

'I had advice about clothes,' said Philippa. 'Athena
chose my dress.' The charm of Phaleron Harbour was
dimmed for her now she knew he had visited it with
Thalia.

'And a very good choice it was,' said Damon. 'I like
that silk, it looks like pale green grass.' She was
dressed in a celadon green shirt dress that swirled
round her hips like water. 'You look like a lovely
mermaid, Pippa—as if you'd joined us from the
water.'

'If I'd joined you from the water I'd be more likely
to be a rat,' Philippa said acidly. 'That water's too
dirty for mermaids.'

Damon didn't answer, he just smiled at her and took

a sip of wine. Athena chattered on about their afternoon's shopping while Philippa watched the waiters scurrying between cars, and tried to regain her good humour. It was so annoying, she thought, that each time she saw Damon now he seemed to grow more attractive. He had met them straight from his office and was still dressed in a navy blue raw-silk business suit. He looked so urbane, so devastatingly handsome, she found it hard not to stare at him in admiration. She remembered that when she had first met him she hadn't found him particularly good-looking, and reflected wryly on the power of love.

'Something on your mind, Pippa?'

She came back to earth with a jolt. 'No . . . no. Just worrying about the waiters,' she lied. 'I was wondering if we'll get our dinner without sacrificing a waiter in the process!' They laughed, and Philippa made an effort to shake off her mood of melancholy, so that by the time their food arrived, miraculously unspilled, she appeared quite normal again.

They finished eating around ten, quite early by Greek standards. When they were driving home Damon said,

'I'm dropping you and Athena off at the apartment, Pippa, I have an appointment.'

'At this hour?' She could have bitten her tongue out as soon as she'd spoken—she sounded exactly like an aggrieved wife!

'In Greece a lot of business is transacted after dinner, Philippa,' Damon told her. 'Besides, the person I want to see won't be available tomorrow.'

He's probably meeting Thalia, Philippa thought miserably, or some other woman. For she now imagined him relentlessly pursuing new conquests, each more beautiful than the last. It's nothing to do with *me*, she counselled herself, but her advice brought no comfort, and she spent a restless night.

Damon was not with them when they left for the ferry the following morning, and she wondered sadly if he had returned to the apartment at all last night.

The ferry looked the size of a respectable ocean liner to Philippa. She leaned on the mahogany rail of the upper deck watching the crowds milling around the quay. Black-clad women clutched small children, impressive-looking priests of the Greek Orthodox Church, their flowing robes and beards whipped by the wind, rubbed shoulders with university students dressed in faded jeans, the uniform of the young all over the world. On the jetty pedlars sold everything from worry beads to pretzel-shaped bread rolls that were threaded on long poles that threatened to knock out the eyes of the unwary.

Idly she watched a crane lower a bright red sports car into the hold. It shone like an exotic scarlet insect in the sunshine. Then she saw Damon striding towards the first class entrance, a good head taller than the Greeks jostling around him. He had changed into casual clothes, and exchanged the navy suit for beige corduroy slacks and a soft suede zippered jacket. He waved when he saw her, and bounded athletically up the gangplank. Seconds later the ship's whistle let out its strident hoot and they were off. People waved and cried, and shouted last-minute messages dramatically. Someone threw paper streamers at the departing ferry, then the ship gathered speed, leaving Piraeus behind, ploughing steadily through the dark blue water towards the enigmatic island of Crete.

Damon arrived at her side, not even slightly out of breath.

'I was beginning to get worried,' she said. 'I thought you'd forgotten us.' Too busy with your mistress to remember your 'pretend wife', she thought to herself.

'The ferry wouldn't have left without me, Pippa. The owner of the line's a friend of mine.'

'I keep forgetting how important you are,' she said, 'it's rather overwhelming sometimes. Very rich for my blood.'

'But you're used to dealing with rich things . . . all that cream and pâté! Why not just relax and enjoy it?' He smiled at her lazily, and she smiled back. For how could anyone nurse a grievance in all this blue air and rushing sea?

'And while we're at it . . .' Damon reached out and unclipped her hair, putting the silver barrette into the pocket of his jacket and zipping it decisively, 'I want to see the wind in your hair,' he said.

'*Damon!*' she cried, laughing as she pushed back her windblown hair from her eyes. She felt suddenly lighthearted, for she realised she would have the whole day with him here on this blessed ferry, where there were no old girl-friends to snatch him away.

Athena rushed on to the deck and nearly fell into Damon's arms. She started chattering excitedly in Greek, then remembering Philippa changed to English.

'Come and see our stateroom, Pippa . . . quickly . . .' she pulled at the unresisting Philippa, 'come on!'

Their stateroom was also on the upper deck, amidships, and when Philippa climbed through the doorway she caught her breath with delight. Every available space was crammed with orchids—great baskets of yellow ones, purple orchids in crystal vases, bunches of pale greenish striped ones, as well as bunches of yellow wallflowers and tall blue iris. On the coffee table was a shallow silver bowl filled with violets.

'A foretaste of Crete,' said Damon. 'We're famous for our orchids, and they'll be finished in a week or so . . . so will the other flowers.'

'They're beautiful, Damon! And violets too. I didn't know violets grew in Crete.'

'They don't. I had those flown in from England . . . in case you were feeling homesick.' For some unaccountable reason he looked shy.

'I'm not a bit homesick, but I love the violets. Thank you!' Philippa was touched that he could be so thoughtful, but a warning voice reminded her that it could also be the ploy of a philanderer. Any man used to seducing women would have a repertiore of such pleasing gestures.

'Oh good—*tiropetas*, delicious!' Athena greeted the steward who entered with a luncheon tray. '*Tiropetas* are cheese tarts, Pippa, I don't think you've tasted them yet.'

'Athena is giving me a gastronomical introduction to Greece,' Philippa laughed. 'Every day I get a new taste sensation. And each one is better than the last.'

Damon opened champagne. He offered a glass to Athena, but she refused, drinking instead her favourite cherry soda.

They soon polished off the *tiropetas*, then ate *dolmades*, vine leaves stuffed with ground meat, rice, and pine nuts, served with yogurt that had a hint of lemon. A dish of nuts and fresh fruit, together with espresso coffee, finished the meal.

Philippa gave a sigh of repletion and stretched out her long legs. She was wearing the white linen slacks and emerald striped shirt she had bought in England.

'Some brandy, Pippa?' Damon asked.

'No, thanks,' Philippa giggled. 'I've had more than enough champagne, I'll sleep all afternoon if I drink any more!'

'Well, I'm sending you both off for a nap now,' Damon said loftily, 'I've a lot of work to do.'

She straightened up in her chair. 'I don't want to go to bed, thank you, Damon,' she said. 'I'm neither drunk nor ill.' Nor about to be bossed around by you, she thought testily.

'I'm not suggesting you're either. But it's a long trip and a rest will do you good. I can't spend any more time entertaining you.'

'I'm not asking you to entertain me. I shall simply have a walk around the ship and entertain myself.' Her tawny eyes glittered with battle.

'You can do all that after you've had a nap.' He turned to his niece, who was watching this clash of wills with fascination. 'Off you go to your cabin, Kookla, and set a good example.' Dutifully Athena left them.

'Honestly, Damon,' Philippa was outraged, 'I must ask you to stop treating me as if I was ten years old! Once and for all, I *don't want to go to bed*!'

He gave an exaggerated sigh of patience. 'Very well, I'll compromise. You will lie on a lounge chair on deck for an hour. Will you agree to *that*?'

'With a book?' she said mutinously.

'With an entire library if you wish.'

'All right. But I think it's ridiculous,' she conceded. She was livid that it was not possible to let him know she resented being ordered around by him, in the face of his cavalier behaviour the previous evening.

A steward was summoned, and she was installed in a cane chair, and wrapped in a light mohair blanket. Damon watched this operation sardonically, then returned to the stateroom to work.

Philippa was awakened two hours later by Damon's velvety voice. 'Tea-time, Pippa. If you sleep any longer you'll miss the sunset.'

The shadows had lengthened and the sea was dark indigo. Philippa got up hurriedly, dropping her unopened book and struggling with the blanket that wound itself round her legs like a mummy's bandages.

'Take it easy, Sleeping Beauty,' Damon cautioned, 'there's no rush. The tea's too weak to walk away from the table.' He untangled the blanket and picked up her book, 'Browning, eh?' he went on, 'Nice light reading when one's not feeling like taking a nap!' She chose to ignore this, and together they went to the stateroom where tea was waiting.

The tea was indeed little more than coloured water, but there was a splendid almond cake to make up for it, and pieces of chopped fruits and nuts that had been dipped in a chocolate so dark they looked black on the white porcelain dish. Blinking sleepily, Philippa drank a cup of the straw-coloured tea, aware of Damon's detached amusement.

Later Philippa stood alone on deck listening to the swish-swish of the ship cutting through the dark water, and watching the sun sink, a glory of cloud-streaked gold. Damon had wrapped the mohair blanket around her shoulders, since the evening air was chill. When dusk fell she became aware of humps of land, silent islands in the surging sea. Sometimes she glimpsed a light winking in the black hills, but for the most part the shapes were unilluminated and sombre. Now the sun had vanished the only brightness visible was the white foam where the ship's prow carved the blue-black sea.

'We'll be docking in Souda Bay about eleven,' Damon's soft voice startled her, she was so caught up in the magic of sea and stars. 'What were you thinking about, Pippa? You seemed miles away ... back in London with Martha?'

'London! ... London seems another world. I wasn't thinking of anything in particular, Damon. Wondering about Chania and Crete ... and the legend of the Minotaur,' she smiled. 'My knowledge of Greek mythology's a bit limited.'

'You must visit Knossos and see the palace, and Phaestos and Mallia. They're all easy to reach from Chania.'

'Is the labyrinth at Knossos?' asked Philippa.

'It was supposed to have been built there to cage the Minotaur, who was causing a lot of trouble for the Minoans. That was King Minos's fault.' Damon's smile gleamed whitely in the darkness. 'If he'd sacrificed the white bull to Poseidon as promised, Poseidon wouldn't have taken revenge on him by making his wife fall in love with the bull.'

'Poseidon's a very impressive-looking god,' Philippa said, 'I wouldn't like to get on the wrong side of him. He reminds me of yo. . . . of someone I know.'

'Well, King Minos got on the wrong side of him all right, and Minos's wife gave birth to the Minotaur, which proceeded to run amok, so it was locked up in the labyrinth. That's all myth, of course, but the early Minoans did practise bull worship. There's a fresco at Knossos of the bull-leaping, which was part of the athletic games that were religious in character too.'

'Bull-leaping? It sounds very dangerous!'

'It was. Boys and girls did it. They literally grasped the bull by the horns, then leapt over his back while he ran at a gallop. I doubt many of them survived.'

'They don't leap over bulls any more in Crete, I hope?' Philippa queried.

'Not any more. But Crete is still the most savage of all the islands. The countryside is very remote, and feuds and vendettas still flourish. Woe betide anyone who dishonours the daughter of a family! A brother will avenge her, and it's not unknown for the betrayer's body to be found floating in the harbour.'

Philippa gave a shiver of apprehension. 'You make it sound most alarming, Damon,' she said. 'I'm not sure I'll enjoy living among such a violent people.'

'You will love Crete, Pippa,' he answered. 'These things do exist, but the Cretans are also the most hospitable people in the world. They're utterly charming.' He gave a small boy's grin. 'After all, I'm half Cretan, and you know what a delightful fellow I am.'

Philippa smiled and remained silent, her imagination alive with Minotaurs and palaces and stormy vendettas. She became aware of lights in the blackness ahead, and a huge island silhouette rose out of the sea.

'We're nearly there,' said Damon, his voice not quite steady. 'That's the harbour. We're home!'

After a while the curve of the bay was clearer, and Philippa could make out cafés, their brilliantly lit interiors like so many fireflies on the quay. There were clusters of people, like ants swarming around, and taxis waiting for the ferry to dock.

'I'd better see about our luggage,' said Damon, making for the stairs.

'Let me help.'

He turned on her sharply, blocking her way. 'Stay where you are, Philippa. You'll only be in the way down there. If you must go anywhere, go to our stateroom till we're docked.' Clearly he considered her a liability. He looked menacing, his bulk filling the narrow doorway that led to the ship's hold.

Hurt, she turned back to the ship's rail. 'I'll stay here, thank you.'

'Well, don't wander about,' he said harshly. 'I've enough to see to without losing you in the crowd.'

She stayed and watched them tie up, blinking tears away from her eyes. Damon always managed to spoil things. Just when a mood of intimacy was created, when they seemed to be in harmony, he would suddenly bark orders at her, brutally reminding her of her real status in his household.

After a while she regained her composure and headed back to the stateroom to join Athena, and get ready to disembark.

Later she and Athena stood together on the teeming jetty waiting for Damon. The crowd milled

around them talking a different kind of Greek from
the liquid sounds she was becoming accustomed to in
Athens. Here the speech was rougher, more guttural.
She noticed that the men were taller than the men on
the mainland, and they all seemed handsome, young
and old, in an aggressively masculine way. Most of
them wore full moustaches, and some had eyes that
were a curious shade of green . . . like the Cretan sea
around them.

Philippa was dazed by the noise and unfamiliar
scents. There was something barbaric about the
crowded harbour, lit by the white lights from the
cafés.

Damon materialised and took charge. 'I'm not
coming to the villa yet, Philippa, I have to supervise
the unloading of . . . supplies . . . from below decks.'
He sounded furtive and Philippa knew he was being
evasive with her. He bundled the two girls into a
waiting Daimler driven by a uniformed chauffeur.
'Don't wait up for me,' he said, 'I shall be late,' then
he returned to the ferry without giving them another
glance.

The drive from Soudan harbour to Damon's house
on the outskirts of Chania was a hectic blur. They
drove fast on the winding road. At each bend the car's
headlights stabbed the steep hillside, and Philippa
noticed great patches of bright purple geraniums
which she later discovered grew wild all over the
island.

Damon's villa was built into the side of a cliff. You
entered the spacious hall and went down stairs to the
living area, then down again to the bedrooms which
opened out on to the garden and the sea beyond.

There were more servants here than in the Athens
apartment. They greeted their new mistress warmly,
and a young girl was presented to her as her personal
maid. Blushing like a peony, the girl led Philippa

down to an enormous bedroom suite. The roughcast
walls were painted white, but woven hangings in
subtle earth tones, warmly tinted watercolours, and
alabaster vases filled with flowers softened any
starkness. On the garden side of the room the entire
wall was composed of sliding glass doors. Now locally
hand-loomed curtains in a soft pattern of dusty pinks,
browns, and white were drawn against the night. The
enormous double bed with its headboard of carved
olive wood was covered in the same soft woollen
fabric.

After Philippa had surveyed her domain she left the
young maid unpacking and returned to the living
room, where Athena, curled up like a kitten in one of
the low modern easy chairs, was yawning her head off.

'If you yawn any wider, Athena, you'll unhinge
your jaw!' smiled Philippa.

'I am so sleepy I cannot see,' the girl admitted.

Philippa suggested bed. 'There's no point waiting
up for Damon—he said he'd be late. And all that sea
air's made me sleepy too.'

On their way to their bedrooms Athena turned to
her. 'You are not angry with Uncle Damon for leaving
you alone your first night here, are you, Pippa?'

'I'm not angry, darling. I'm sure he had a good
reason to stay behind,' Philippa assured her.

But when she was brushing her honey-beige hair
she wondered what that reason could be. He had
seemed so shifty when he had left them, she couldn't
help thinking it more than likely he had a meeting
with some woman. Whatever the reason she was too
tired to fret about. Moreover, it was good discipline. It
would serve to remind her that what Damon did with
his private life had nothing to do with her.

The routine at the villa was different from that in
Athens, she discovered. Her maid brought her tea, put
out the clothes she planned to wear, then breakfast was

served on the patio. Philippa bathed hastily and stepped through the glass doors into a world of breathtaking beauty ablaze with sunshine. The garden was on three levels. The first level had an oval swimming pool surrounded by a wooden deck. Here tubs of brightly coloured flowers jostled against sunloungers, striped beach umbrellas, and high-backed wicker armchairs. There was also a portable bar and a change-room for guests, and to the right of this was a paved patio. Here stood a glass-topped table under a pale blue awning. This was set for breakfast.

Steps had been cut into the cliff face to lead down to the second level. Here was a partly cultivated garden, skilfully landscaped so that none of the wild charm of the place was sacrificed. Two dark spiky cypresses stood sentinel over the next set of steps, which led to a small grove of olive trees and a businesslike-looking vegetable garden. At the bottom of this garden, shimmering in the early morning sun like a newly cut turquoise, was the sea. A small sailing boat and a motor launch were moored at a sizeable concrete jetty, and a diving board was clamped to the rocks.

Philippa stood in the lower garden, hypnotised by the sound of the sea slapping against the rocks, and the shrill call of gulls wheeling overhead. The sun caressed her bare arms and set shafts of silver dancing in her hair. She stood very still for a long time, then she heard Athena calling her, and she roused herself from her sundrenched dream.

'Pippa, hurry!' the girl urged as Philippa climbed up to the top level. 'I am very hungry for breakfast, and there is a present for you.'

'A present? Where?'

'Look!' Athena pointed to a pot of flowering basil sitting on the table. There was a note propped against it in Damon's firm hand. Philippa broke the seal and read:

'Pippa—In Greece a sprig of flowering basil is given as a token of friendship. Look in the pot and you will find the second token. The third token is on the driveway. It is a mortal insult to refuse a gift from a Greek!—Damon.'

She looked in the pot as instructed and found a key stuck in the soil. It was a car key, with the name 'Ferrari' stamped on the scarlet leather. It dangled from her fingers, glinting in the light.

'Do not just *stand there*, Pippa!' said Athena, smiling conspiratorially. 'Come!' Taking Philippa's hand, she led her to the front door, and opened it dramatically, 'Look!' she exclaimed.

There, glittering on the white marble driveway, stood the scarlet sports car Philippa had watched being lowered into the hold of the ferry.

'It is a present from Uncle Damon—a present for *you*,' Athena went on when Philippa remained speechless. 'Quickly, Pippa! Let us eat some breakfast, and then we shall go for a drive—yes?' she implored.

Philippa nodded. Things were falling into place. Last night Damon must have stayed at the docks in order to drive the car home, not to keep a date as she had suspected. That also explained why he had brusquely refused her offer to help with the unloading of the luggage. It was an overwhelming gesture, and she was pleased, of course . . . and yet . . . she couldn't help feeling he had also pulled a fast one. She had made it clear she wouldn't accept his offer of a new car that morning at his lawyer's. Besides, she felt obligated to him now. She didn't like that. She wasn't sure she knew how she was going to deal with this.

The two girls spent most of the morning driving around the coast road. The car handled well, and Philippa enjoyed the feel of its controlled power, like a barely tamed animal, under her hands. At noon they drove into the town of Chania, which was an ancient honey-coloured town of Venetian style. It boasted a cruciform market in its centre, and a small harbour ringed by the inevitable tavernas. The morning's catch of squid was strung out to dry in the sun. Athena pointed to the far end of the old harbour, where a spur of land jutted out into the sea.

'Uncle Damon's hotel is just round that corner,' she said.

'Let's pay him a visit, then,' Philippa suggested. Maybe inspiration would strike and she would think of a way to thank him, while letting him know that she hadn't been taken in.

They parked the vivid little car at the bottom of the hill and walked the rest of the way. To their left lay the sparkling expanse of blue water, and to their right, soaring above the town, were the snow-capped peaks of the mountains which ran down the length of Crete like a rocky spine.

Damon's hotel looked deceptively small, and blended in so well with the landscape that at first it was hardly noticeable. Like his villa it was built on various levels, and was constructed of granite. Workmen were busy putting last-minute touches to the place. Gardeners were planting tubs and window-boxes with flowers. Inside, painters were finishing the plaster-covered walls, which were being decorated with copies of frescos from early Minoan palaces.

Athena spoke to one of the workmen, then guided Philippa towards the kitchens. Philippa, long-legged and golden in blue jeans and shirt, was aware of the approving stares of the local workmen as she picked her way through the paintpots and plaster.

The kitchens were vast, and unlike the rest of the hotel looked very modern. They gleamed with stainless steel. Gigantic counters and working islands flanked stoves which looked like the instrument panels of a jet. Damon was standing in the centre of the room, a sheaf of blueprints in his hand. When he saw Philippa and his niece he smiled a welcome.

'Why, Pippa, what a nice surprise!'

'I didn't mean to interrupt your work, Damon,' Philippa apologised, 'but I couldn't wait till this evening to thank you for your present.'

'Are you not going to kiss him?' Athena asked.

'Of course I am,' Philippa replied, chastely planting a kiss on his lean brown cheek. Damon gave a chuckle and caught her to him in a hug that set her senses reeling. He released her and she surreptitiously held the counter for support. The feel of his powerful body against hers turned her knees to rubber.

'You like your new toy, then?' he asked.

'Of course I like it, but . . . but . . .'

'But? But what . . .?' He turned to Athena, 'It's lunch time, Kookla,' he said, 'why don't you go down to our usual taverna and hold a table for us? I'll treat you both to lunch.'

'Ooh, lovely!' Athena's eyes sparkled. 'Can I have moussaka?'

'Certainly. But be sure to phone the villa and let the servants know you won't be lunching at home. Off you go!' Athena sped away, and Philippa was alone in the vast kitchen with her husband. 'Now, Pippa,' he said, 'why all the "buts"? Is the car the wrong colour?'

'No, of course not. But I thought we decided in London that you wouldn't buy me a car?' This sounded so ungracious she tried to make it sound better, and only succeeded in making it worse. 'I mean, it's too . . . too expensive for . . . for a gift, and it's not . . . not in the contract . . .'

His face looked suddenly drawn, as if a cloud had passed over the sun.

'Always the business woman, eh, Pippa?' he sighed, 'but not always very bright. The car is for your use while you're in Crete, to enable you to amuse Athena. When you return to England you will leave it here.'

Philippa turned fiery red—how could she have been so stupid? Of course, it was not really a gift at all.

'Bu—but the *way* you gave it to me, with the pot of basil, and ... I thought ...' She wished she could crawl into a hole somewhere, away from the frosty gaze of his blue eyes.

'Merely putting on an act for Athena's benefit,' he said harshly. 'We are supposed to be newlyweds.'

'I ... I've been very dense ... I'm sorry, Damon, I ...'

He broke in roughly, 'Now forget it, Philippa. It's not important. I want you to take a quick tour of the kitchen, then you can give me your valuable opinion. I might as well cash in on the fact that your main interest seems to lie in being first and foremost a professional ... cook!'

She recoiled at the venom in his voice, then recovered her poise and started examining the kitchen in detail, opening oven doors, and inspecting refrigerators, conscious of him leaning against the doorway following her with angry eyes.

She asked pertinent questions, surprised that her voice sounded controlled, and grateful that she was far enough away to hide her trembling hands. At last she finished her inspection and turned to him. He looked so haughty leaning against the door, unapproachable, a different being from the one who had joked with Athena a few minutes ago.

'I think your kitchen's perfect, Damon,' she said.

'Do you?' He managed to make it sound contemptuous.

'Apart from one thing.'

'Indeed?'

She ignored the sneer in his tone. 'The working islands should be on casters,' he looked at her, 'so they can be moved easily from one area to another, or pushed aside when they're not needed. It would be much more efficient.' Sunlight bounced off the stainless steel fittings, and motes of dust spun, trapped in beams of light. Philippa could hear her own quiet breath in the still kitchen.

Weariness replaced the anger in his face. 'That's not a bad suggestion,' he said, 'I might try it. Now we'd better join Athena before she gets worried.'

Silently they walked down the hill to the harbour, Damon's long legs taking such strides Philippa was hard put to it to keep up with him. They passed the car where she had parked it, and she felt such a pang of regret for the clumsy way she had handled everything a lump came to her throat. When they neared the half-moon of cafés he took her arm. There was no intimacy in his grasp, and she realised miserably that this gesture was for appearances' sake only.

Athena was sitting at one of the tavernas sipping cherry soda. She waved gaily when she saw them. 'Do hurry!' she cried, 'I am so hungry I could eat the chairs! I ordered taramasalata for us to start with,' she told Damon when they had sat down.

'A good idea, Kookla, but I'm not very hungry,' he replied, 'that will be all I'll want.'

'That's all I want too,' said Philippa, and Athena looked at her in surprise, 'I'm not hungry either,' she explained.

'Oho! So it is true, then?' Athena attacked her bread with gusto.

'What's true?' asked Damon.

'That people in love lose their appetites.'

'It's easy to see you're not in love,' Damon snapped. 'For goodness' sake don't gobble bread like that, Athena, you'll get indigestion!' Moodily he poured some mineral water into a glass.

Conversation lagged, and when the fish pâté arrived ceased altogether. Even Athena's ebullient mood took a nosedive in the black atmosphere. The two adults morosely watched her plough her way through a plate of creamy mousaka, then silently Damon paid the bill and the three of them walked back to the bright little car.

'I love Pippa's new car, Uncle Damon. When did you get it?' asked Athena, attempting to break the oppressive mood.

'I got it in Athens our last night there,' he told her. 'The dealer only returned from a trip then. I drove it down to Piraeus myself at three in the morning.'

Climbing into the driver's seat of the sporty little car, Philippa felt worse than ever. Why had he gone to such immense trouble? If it was, technically, just an extra vehicle for a member of the staff, why not get any old car in Chania? He wanted to present a picture of a happy marriage to Athena, she supposed, but it seemed rather excessive behaviour. She would never understand him.

'I won't be home for dinner tonight,' Damon said to Phillipa in the cutting tone he might use to a dimwitted member of his staff.

'Very well.' She started the engine and drove away fast, leaving him standing in a cloud of dust.

'I'm afraid I've annoyed your uncle,' she said lightly to Athena.

The girl pulled a comical little face.

'He is in one of his moods. But it will not last, Pippa. He has a terrible temper,' she added with evident relish, 'and when he loses it he feels ashamed and becomes silent. He will be perfectly all right in an hour or so, you will see.' She turned her clear gaze on Philippa. It was plain she had no misgivings about her uncle.

But Philippa didn't feel so sanguine. She knew she

had wounded him, had hurt his pride, and she cursed herself for the rest of the long day that she could have been so thoughtless. For she was discovering that to hurt someone you love was worse than being hurt yourself. That the pain of being unable to reach out and comfort him tore her in two, and drew all pleasure from the luminous beauty that surrounded her.

# CHAPTER NINE

THE golden days fell into a routine. Philippa would swim each morning in the oval swimming pool, then eat breakfast with Athena. Sometimes Damon would join them, but usually he was gone by seven. After their meal of fruit, bread, and honey the two girls would lie in the sun for an hour while Athena gave Philippa a lesson in Greek. Philippa loved this part of the day. She was an apt pupil, and enjoyed mastering phrases and using them at every opportunity.

After her lesson she showered and dressed, then visited the kitchen, accompanied by her phrase book, to discuss the day's menu with the chef. Then she and Athena would climb into the little red car and explore Crete.

They rarely ate lunch at the villa, preferring to take a simple picnic with them, and sit under the shadow of a gnarled olive tree enjoying the heavenly scent of wild dittany, Crete's native herb, which mingled delightfully with the smell of honeysuckle, thyme and salt sea air. Replete after their picnic, Philippa would lie back on the herb-scented ground, listening to the bleating of goats on the hillside, drifting between dozing and waking, and falling deeper in love with Damon and his native land each day.

May advanced; Damon's Chania project was nearly completed, and soon he would be spending all his time in Herakleion. At the end of the following week he planned the grand opening of the Chania hotel, and he asked Philippa to arrange a reception for seventy at the villa, prior to the formal party at the hotel. She set about this task with enthusiasm, grateful to have a chance to work. It helped to take her mind off her obsessive need for Damon, which was beginning to crowd out all other thoughts and pleasures.

She discussed possible cocktail snacks with the chef, and after several interviews, aided by much gesticulating and hand language, they fixed on a menu. She noted with satisfaction the unmistakable look of respect in the chef's eyes, the respect of one professional for another. It was gratifying to know she hadn't lost her touch in the kitchen.

Athena's friend from the ferry crossing had turned up again. The girl's family had rented a house in a village just outside Chania. Athena spent a lot of time with them, so Philippa had a chance to explore on her own. She wandered through tiny villages perched high on the cliffside, she clambered over ancient ruins and daydreamed over their timeworn secrets. She discovered orange groves, where smiling labourers offered her bags full of the juicy fruit, gifts to the blonde stranger in their midst. She spent lazy afternoons swimming from deserted beaches, and tanned herself to a lovely golden brown.

After one such afternoon she returned to the villa to find Damon seated by the pool drinking coffee, his lean body stretched out on one of the gaily striped lounge chairs. As usual when she met him unexpectedly her heart gave a jolt, and her hands became unsteady.

'You're home early,' she said brightly, hoping her smile looked impersonal and did not give away the tumultous joy she felt at seeing him.

'Mmm. Things seem pretty much under control for the next few days. Nothing for me to do until the official opening,' he told her. 'How's the reception coming along?'

Philippa told him the food she planned to serve, and the flower arrangements. It felt strange, sitting overlooking the aquamarine sea of Crete, cypresses stabbing into the incredibly blue sky, discussing menus with him just as she had months ago in London. Only then she had not held her hands together tightly so that he wouldn't notice them tremble, nor kept her long-lashed eyes down because to look too long into his deep blue ones could lead her to giving away her precious, painful secret.

'It all sounds most professional, Pippa,' he said. 'And now I propose we take a short holiday—what do you say?'

She reached for one of the sweet biscuits on the coffee tray. 'A holiday? I feel as if I've been having nothing *but* a holiday since I arrived.'

'While I've been slaving!' His eyes twinkled with amusement. 'Then I shall pull rank and request that you spend the next twenty-four hours as *my* companion, since Athena seems to have deserted you.'

She nodded coolly, and bit into the biscuit, hoping to hide the flush of pleasure that warmed her cheek.

'Have you visited the Gorge of Samara yet, Pippa?' he asked. She hadn't, although she'd heard about the world famous gorge, with its subterranean river and long narrow path to the sea. 'Then tomorrow let's hike down the gorge together. Would you like that?' She nodded. 'It's eighteen kilometres of rough terrain. Think you're up to it?'

She rose to the bait. 'Certainly! I'm probably in better shape than you.'

He laughed. 'Don't tempt fate, Pippa. *Hubris* is a dangerous thing to call down on yourself. We'll take the early bus to Omalos and backpack to Roumeli—do it properly, like tourists. We can take the last boat back to the mainland.'

That evening Philippa organised food for them to take next day. She checked her walking shoes. Damon had warned her that they would be fording the river in some places, and an extra pair of sneakers was essential.

Athena declined to go with them, as she had seen the gorge before, and her friend's older brother had promised to take them sailing tomorrow—a far more attractive prospect to a teenager than slogging for eighteen kilometres with relatives. Guiltily Philippa was overjoyed by her refusal. She loved Athena, but tomorrow the old axiom 'two's company, three's a crowd!' seemed particularly apt.

She rose at four the following morning, and crept into the dark kitchen to make coffee. She found Damon there, and they talked in whispers so as not to disturb the sleeping household. She felt like a child on Christmas morning, full of excitement at the promise of the day to come. Damon rooted around in the fridge looking for extra lemons to take, organising the backpack. He seemed like a boy at the prospect of their day.

As they were leaving he looked at her outfit critically and sent her back to fetch a warmer sweater, warning her that it was cold in the mountains before the sun was high. He was wearing faded jeans, a disreputable old denim shirt, and battered sneakers. For warmth he wore his elegant fawn suede jacket over this shabby get-up, which struck an incongruous note.

She hastily pulled on a thick scarlet sweater and at four-thirty a.m. they were off.

They drove in Philippa's little car to the bus station in Chania, left it there and climbed into the shabby bus with a few other intrepid tourists. It was still pitch dark outside, but when they had been climbing for a while the first streaks of dawn, like bronze metal in the early morning sky, sent warm pencils of light on to the lush, fertile scenery around them. The sun grew stronger. They reached a picturesque village of red-roofed houses with white walls, which seemed to tumble down the mountainside. The road wound in a crazy zig-zag high into the snow-capped peaks beyond. Sometimes the bus would stop in the middle of nowhere and a shepherd would climb aboard, usually dressed in the old-fashioned Cretan garb of loose breeches tucked into high leather boots, a cummerbund wound round his waist, and a black silk headscarf with small tassles that swung on his forehead, and set off to perfection the wrinkled brown skin of his handsome face.

The bus started to fill up—more shepherds, some carrying lambs, a few goatherds, and another passenger with a crate of chickens. The bus driver put on the tape-deck at full blast, and bouzouki music vied with the bleating and the clucking, and the various conversations in rapid Greek, all carried on at full volume.

Damon slumped in the aisle seat, seemingly asleep. But once Philippa turned to look at him and his eyes were open. He was regarding her intently.

'Do you like it so far, Pippa?'

'Yes—oh yes!'

'Good.' He closed his eyes and seemed to doze.

The bus drove through bleak stony uplands with stunted fir trees to an enclosed pass, then made a short steep descent to where the plain lay spread out below.

Omalos—one of the most impressive of Crete's upland plains. It looked to Philippa like a vast drained lake. There was no village in this barren place, merely a couple of tumbledown cottages that leaned precariously into the wind. The bus drove steadily across this vast wasteland to the far end, where it drew up with a flourish outside the Tourist Pavilion and the entrance to the gorge.

Damon picked up the backpack and helped Philippa climb down, for she was stiff after two hours cramped in the bus. The air struck her face like crystal, sharp and cold.

'Before we have breakfast, Pippa, come and look at this,' he said, leading her to the wooden staircase that led down to the gorge below.

The golden sun glanced over dark green fir trees that clung to the thin skin of soil covering the towering crags. At the bottom of the gorge she could see the tops of cypress and pine trees waving in the breeze like a deep green sea. A spume of water thundered a thousand feet down into the unseen river below. On three sides the breathtaking view of the White Mountains spread as far as the eye could see.

The splendour made her catch her breath. 'Oh, Damon, it's . . . it's fantastic.' She was mesmerised by the strange brooding beauty of the place.

He chuckled with satisfaction. 'Come on Pippa, breakfast—get a move on!' he said, and guided her, reluctantly, to the Tourist Pavilion.

They ate a peasant breakfast of crusty rolls, goats butter, and Nescafé, then he shouldered the pack and they set off.

It took half an hour to climb the one kilometre down the wooden steps to the footpath which followed the shallow river, crossing it at times, where it bubbled up from its underground bed. On all sides shrubs and sweet herbs grew. The scent of dittany and thyme mixed with wild honeysuckle and aromatic rock plants was overpowering.

At noon they stopped to rest and eat their picnic. Damon chose a small sandy bay shaded with pines. The sun was now blazing down, they had long since discarded sweaters and jackets, and Philippa lay thankfully in the dappled shadows. They ate the lunch she had prepared the previous night, tomatoes and cheeses, hardboiled eggs and juicy oranges. Damon filled two thermos mugs with the sweet mountain water and squeezed lemons into it, then handed her one.

'Here, Pippa, I think this is the best drink in the world. Try it.'

She sipped the tart water, it was so icy it seemed to bubble against her lips. She was hot and pleasantly tired, and this special kind of lemonade tasted better than any wine would have done.

'It's wonderful,' she said. 'So is all this,' she gestured to the surrounding mountains, the tumbling water, the blue sky arching high above them.

'I thought you'd like it.' He sounded happy. 'And now I suggest an hour's rest before we tackle the rest of our journey.'

Philippa lay back on the silvery sand, listening to the rapid torrent, feeling the soft mountain breeze cool on her face.

'Put your head on this.' Damon rolled up his suede jacket and tucked it under her head, then he stretched his long body out several feet away from her. 'Whoever wakes first wakes the other. O.K?'

She lay, her cheek pillowed on the soft leather of his jacket which gave off a faint aroma of his special cologne, aromatic, subtle. She fought against sleep, for she wanted to store every minute of this special day with him in her memory—a special memory for the empty years ahead. But sleep overcame her at last, and when she woke an hour later she was glad of it, for she felt as refreshed as if she had slept a full eight hours.

The river grew broader, and the path crossed and re-crossed it crazily, sometimes by a series of slippery stepping-stones. But more often they would plunge through the knee-high, cold green water, laughing, splashing, childishly enjoying the sensation of squelching around in wet running shoes.

The last part of their walk took them through the

*sidheroportes*, or 'iron gates', the narrowest part of the gorge. The cliffs rose sheer nearly a thousand feet, and the walls of the gorge were only a few feet wide. The river had disappeared underground now, and they climbed over immense boulders that choked the dry bed. No sunlight reached here; the only brightness was the narrow slice of blue sky above. Philippa was glad when they left that part behind and reached the plain. The river bubbled forth again, and magenta-coloured rhododendrons bloomed on each side of the path.

Turning a corner, they saw their first glimpse of the sea and within minutes they were sitting at the primitive taverna on the beach, drinking coffee and congratulating themselves on their good timing.

'We've three hours before the boat comes,' Damon said. 'Did you bring a swimsuit?'

'Naturally. I wouldn't dream of moving in Crete without one.'

'The beach is stony, but the swimming's good. We can change in the caves at the end of the bay. Are you game?'

Philippa changed into her white one-piece, and met him by the shore. It was not the first time she had seen him in swim trunks, and she admired again his taut muscular body, the crisp hair curling on his broad chest. His powerful shoulders gleamed dark brown in the sunshine like polished wood.

'A lot of local people think early May too soon for swimming, Pippa,' he said, 'they only go in when the water's steaming. I imagine you're made of sterner stuff?' He cocked his eyebrow quizzically.

'I'll have you know I've bathed in the English Channel in early May,' she replied, pinning up her hair while she looked up at him.

'Then a spartan like you will have no problem going in.' He grabbed her hand and started pulling her towards the water. It felt chill on her legs at first.

She yelped, 'No! Damon ... no ... let's go in *gradually* ...' but he kept pulling her, laughing, protesting, into the deeper water. Then he gave her a sudden push and she fell in with a splash. She surfaced, spluttering, pushing her wet hair out of her eyes.

'Damon, you rat ... just you wait!' She swam to where he floated a few feet away, then dived and grasped his ankles, dunking him unceremoniously. They played like carefree children, splashing each other, trying to pull each other down into the translucent depths. Then they rested, floating on their backs, admiring the mountains in the distance, capped in winter white. Eventually they struck out for the shore. Philippa had no difficulty keeping pace with him, for she was a strong swimmer. But she hated to leave this world of water and sky where she and Damon seemed to lose the inhibitions of grown-ups and could clown like a couple of kids.

Back on the beach she shook out her dripping hair, wrapped a towel round her head, then lay down on her stomach to finish drying off.

'That's a nice tan you've acquired, Pippa,' said Damon, 'but don't be fooled by the afternoon sun. It's still strong. Better put some oil on if you don't want to burn.'

She reached for their pack and pulled out a tube of protective cream.

'Here, let me.' He took the tube from her and knelt beside her. 'Pull your straps down so I can get to your shoulders.' Silently she undid the narrow shoestring straps and tied them in front of her suit. He began massaging the oily cream on to her back with slow firm strokes, his hands caressing her supple skin.

Philippa lay rigid on the hot pebbles. The touch of his hand awoke feelings in her she didn't know she possessed. She felt as if her whole body, lying defenceless under his ministrations, told him with every pulse-beat of her longing for him. She buried her flushed face in her arms and lay absolutely still, praying her treacherous flesh would not betray her.

He toyed with a tendril of her damp hair, tucked it up into her towel-turban, then abruptly turned away, replaced the cap on the tube of cream and carelessly threw it on to the pack.

'You're done,' he said, opening a magazine and turning his back on her. Philippa lay still, trying to control the trembling of her body. When she could finally trust herself to speak she asked him,

'What's that ruin at the top of the cliff?'

'An old Venetian fort. I climbed up there once. There's nothing much to see, apart from the view, and you've had plenty of views today.'

'I'd like to look at it just the same,' she said, gathering her clothes, 'I've got time before the boat, haven't I?'

She had to remove herself from him for a while. His presence, so masculine lying beside her on this stony beach, tormented her to distraction. She needed to put distance between them.

'I don't recommend it, Philippa.' He turned over on his side to look at her, his eyes vivid with disapproval. 'You've been walking all day.'

She started towards the cave. 'I'm going to do it just the same,' she threw over her shoulder at him,' who knows if I'll ever get a chance again?'

Hurriedly she dressed and braided her damp hair into a single plait. When she returned to the beach Damon was dressed himself, and she wondered if he intended to come with her.

'While you tire yourself out climbing I mean to sit in the taverna and enjoy a drink,' he said. 'I think you're crazy, but I suppose, apart from physically restraining you, I can't stop you. You won't reconsider this particular piece of idiocy?'

'Nope! I'll be as quick as I can,' she replied lightly.

She left him at the taverna and started up the narrow path to the clifftop. The heat was like an arrow, and soon her light shirt was sticking to her back. The cool swim with Damon seemed an age away. Halfway up she nearly gave up this project and turned back, for the path disappeared, and she had to climb up the baked side of the rocks hand over hand. At times a ribbon-thin goat track would emerge, but this was so powdery and dangerous she was forced to crawl up it on her hands and knees.

By the time she reached the summit she was cursing herself. Putting distance between herself and Damon hadn't worked anyway. The memory of those few minutes when he had touched her, and her body had melted under his careless caress was as vivid as ever.

She looked round the small ruin, which wasn't worth the climb, then turned her attention to the view. This was spectacular! The gorge was to her left, a savage ravine in the cliffs, mountains stretched to the right, and before her was the sea. Below she could see the roof of the little taverna, and outside a blue dot was sitting at a table, that was Damon enjoying his drink. A little boat was pulling into the harbour . . . a *boat* . . . the boat back to the mainland!

Philippa jumped to her feet and hastily started to climb down the cliff path, slipping and sliding on the loose shingle. She reached the part where the path disintegrated without mishap, tried to gain a grip on the steep sun-baked rock, when her ankle gave way, and she fell, tumbling down the cliff face for about twenty feet, scratching her arms and legs, grasping desperately until finally she came to rest against a small shrub which grew tenatiously out of the parched earth.

Hanging on to the plant for grim death, she regained her breath, and waited for her shattered nerves to calm. Still holding fast to her shrub, she stretched out her long legs to search for a foothold. A stab of pain shot through her right ankle, and with dismay she realised she had twisted it. She pushed with her good foot until she'd managed to get into a more secure position on the narrow ledge. She was desperately trying not to panic, and wondered if she could slide down the rest of the way on her bottom, but her nerve had failed her, and the thought of leaving the security of the ledge was too much.

Looking down at the hamlet, still so far beneath her, made her dizzy. She noticed that the blue dot that was Damon had disappeared. Perhaps he was already sitting in the boat, waiting impatiently for her to join him. What would he do when she didn't turn up? How long would she be forced to sit here before she was missed?

She knew now she had been mad to attempt such a climb after a long day's hike . . . mad and stubborn. But the need to escape him had driven her, and now she was stuck on this wretched cliff for the Lord knew how long, with a rapidly swelling right ankle that was starting to throb painfully.

'Pippa . . . Pippa, are you all right?'

Damon's voice! He wan't sitting waiting on the boat after all. Gingerly she leaned forward and peered down. The top of his dark head was several feet below her.

'Da—Damon, I'm here—on a ledge.' Her eyes filled with tears of relief. 'I . . . I can't move.'

'Don't panic, I'm coming. Are you hurt?' He was steadily climbing towards her.

'Just my ankle. I think I must have sprained it.'

'Don't worry, Pippa.'

'Oh. I'm not in the least bit worried,' she gasped, 'just enjoying the view.'

'I can think of better places to do that.' There was a rattle of shale as his weight dislodged a stone, then with a heave he was sitting beside her. 'Mind if I join you?' he grinned ironically.

'Be my guest ... I've never been so glad to see anyone,' she admitted with a shaky smile.

'That's what I like, proper appreciation,' he teased. 'And the ruin? Did it come up to your expectations?'

'No, it didn't. Most disappointing.'

'I suppose it wouldn't be gentlemanly to say I told you so!'

'It would be justified,' Philippa said ruefully.

At that moment she noticed the boat draw away from the jetty and start steaming along the coast, away from Roumeli.

'Oh, Damon, the boat!' she cried.

'Yes, we've missed it,' he said mildly.

'I'm ... I'm so sorry, Damon, it's all my fault.'

'Don't worry about it. Our first concern is to get you down safely. Let's look at your ankle. You're sure it's nothing worse than a sprain?' He felt her ankle gently. 'It's not broken at any rate. Now, Pippa, put your arms round my neck and I'll take your weight and slide you down to the path. O.K.?'

'I won't be too heavy for you?'

'Depends how much baklava you've been indulging in lately.' He smiled into her troubled hazel eyes. 'I'm quite a big boy, Pippa, I think I can manage.'

She did as he asked, putting her arms round his neck, helping him slide her down the slope. He clung to what little ledges and footholds he could find, and slowly eased her towards the path. Her ankle caught sometimes and she gave a grimace, but she bit her lip and stifled any sound of pain.

Finally they reached the path and the last part of the descent. Damon sat her on the edge of the pathway and crouched beside her. The sun was now a dark gold. It would soon be sunset, and then dusk would fall like a silken veil around them.

'Let's have a small rest, shall we?' said Damon. He sounded perfectly content, not at all annoyed at missing the boat.

'Damon, I'm terribly sorry about all this,' Philippa sighed, 'it's all my fault. I shouldn't have gone up to the ruin—you were quite right. I ... I don't know what to say ...'

'Don't worry so, Pippa. I'll phone the mainland from the taverna, and they'll send another boat for us.'

'And when we get to the mainland? What then? We'll have missed the last bus.'

'Then I'll phone Chania and get them to drive out for us. Now will you please stop worrying!'

'I still feel awful about it.'

'Well, don't! Look on it as a small penance from the gods to pay for such a lovely day. I'm only sorry you've hurt your ankle.' He smiled at her, one of his heartwarming smiles that always flooded her with joy. 'Now sit still and enjoy the view like a good girl, and stop all this guilt.'

Philippa smiled, and then relaxed, enjoying the warm scented evening. Looking at the dark sea, smelling the fragrance of crushed thyme, she mused that she would never fathom him. She had expected to receive the full brunt of his temper, and in all honesty she wouldn't have blamed him. Instead he was gentle and hadn't uttered a single reproach. She would never understand him.

After a while he rose and stooped over her. 'Hang on to me, Pippa,' he said, 'I'm going to carry you down now.' Without waiting for her answer he picked her up in his arms and calmly walked down the mountain path as if she had been no heavier than a bundle of feathers.

She nestled in his arms, her lips a kiss away from

the brown hollow of his throat. She could see how the hair grew along the side of his neck and curled softly behind his ear. At first she resolutely kept her head tense, but she was very tired, and the temptation to lay her cheek against the base of his throat and relax in his strong safe arms was too great. With a small sigh she abandoned herself to this heaven, praying he would attribute this surrender to shock and fatigue.

As far as she was concerned they reached the taverna all too soon. The proprietor and his wife reacted to their arrival dramatically, and there was much wringing of hands and general concern. Damon laid her in one of the battered easy chairs on the back verandah. The proprietor's wife went scuttering off for a bucket of icy water and some torn-up rags to bind Philippa's ankle. *Raki* was produced, and Philippa was left with her foot soaking in the water, a brimming glass of local brew in her hand, while Damon went to arrange about a boat. She sipped the *Raki*, then diplomatically put it to one side. It tasted like diesel oil and had a kick like a mule. After a little while Damon returned.

'We've run into a bit of a problem, Pippa,' he told her, 'it seems they can't send us a boat after all.'

'What will we do?'

'Stay here overnight and catch the first boat back in the morning.'

'Can they put us up?'

'Oh yes. I phoned Chania, so they won't worry. Er . . . there is one other problem though,' he didn't look particularly worried.

'What's that?'

'There's only one guest room. We'll have to share a room tonight.'

'OH!'

'I know that's not in the contract, Pippa,' he said lightly, 'but I'll behave like a perfect gentleman. I'll let you have the bed and I'll sleep on the floor.' She remained silent. 'There's nothing else we can do, my dear. We're stranded.' He refrained from pointing out that it was her fault.

'Yes . . . I do see,' she said.

'Now I'll see what I can do about rustling up some dinner. I don't know about you but I'm ravenous. Oh, and Pippa,' he reached out and started unbraiding her hair, 'your pigtail's fine for scrambling around mountains, but you're down now.'

She sat motionless, her dust-stained jeans rolled up, her sprained foot inelegantly soaking in a bucket of water, while he gently combed out her long sun-streaked hair. He stood back and looked at her.

'Your hair is the colour of moonlight,' he said softly. 'You're very beautiful Pippa.'

'Especially with my foot in a bucket,' she said, smiling. 'Damon, you're being awfully nice about all this. I do appreciate it.'

'Then show your appreciation by enjoying the rest of our holiday and stop apologising all the time. I'll carry you upstairs in a bit and you can wash before dinner.' He sounded like the old Damon again, crisp and bossy. And while this was safer she treasured the glimpse he had shown her of the other, softer side of him.

Later, washed and dusted off, her foot bound in the torn sheet their landlady provided, they sat outside and ate dinner, which was simple but good—home-baked bread, a dip of chick peas laced with garlic, a grilled fish, caught by their host that afternoon, and sugary halva, like a beautiful slice of marble on the rough pottery dish. They had drunk harsh white wine, poured from an unlabelled bottle, and now they sipped Metaxa brandy with their coffee. Listening to the rhythmic sound of the sea washing over the pebbled shore, Philippa felt utterly at peace. All her guards

were down and she had no defences now. She and
Damon hardly spoke, but the rapport between them
was better than words.

Their host came out and said something to Damon,
who drained his glass and turning to Philippa said,

'It's time to call it a day, Pippa. They've left a lamp
in our room. If you've finished your brandy I'll carry
you up.' He ignored her protests that she was perfectly
capable of walking, and lifted her again in his powerful
arms and carried her easily up the narrow staircase to
the small bedroom that looked out over the beach. An
oil lamp was standing on the rough dresser, casting a
warm light over the whitewashed walls. He laid her
gently on to the double bed. Still leaning over her, he
said huskily,

'How does your ankle feel now, Pippa?' His
proximity was so overpowering she found it difficult
to answer.

'Fi—fine, thank you . . . it doesn't ache at all any
more.' His face in the steady glow of the oil lamp
looked as if it was carved from fine grained wood. He
reached out and tenderly pushed her hair away from
her face.

'Pippa . . . Pippa, you're so beautiful,' he said
hoarsely, 'so lovely.'

He gave a moan and brought his mouth down on
hers in a long kiss, but this time his lips were gentle,
not angry, caressing, lulling her. Philippa's mouth
opened like a flower under his. A sense of delicious
languor filled her and her breath quickened. She was
conscious of nothing but the sound of the surf
whispering outside, and the urgency of his compelling
mouth.

With the lightness of a butterfly's wing Damon
undid the buttons of her shirt and she felt his fingers
on her warm flesh. When he cupped her breast desire
shot through her like a flame. Forgetting all caution,

she abandoned herself, throwing her arms around him, pulling him down to her. He lay beside her and held her tight against him, raining her neck and shoulders with light kisses, uttering broken endearments. His fingers, clumsy now with passion, fumbled with the waistband of her jeans.

'Pippa, I want you so ... I want you so badly ...' He undid the zipper on her jeans and started to stroke her flat stomach, kissing her neck and earlobe. 'I want you, Pippa ... I want you ...'

The repetition of this phrase brought Philippa from the brink of surrender. That he wanted her ardently she had no doubt, and she certainly had made it plain that she felt the same; with one subtle difference. She loved him as passionately as she desired him, but he had made no mention of the word love. He *wanted* her, she inflamed him. But so had countless others. But he did not love her, and without his love she could not give herself to him.

Using every last ounce of will-power left she put both hands against his chest and pushed him away.

'No! Damon ... no. Please ... I ... I can't! Please stop!' She pulled herself away from him, wincing when a stab of pain shot through her damaged ankle, and sat trembling on the far side of the bed.

Slowly he swung himself up to a sitting position, his breath rasping. 'What do you mean? You can't?'

'I ... can't.' She buttoned her shirt over her naked breasts. 'I ... I'm terribly sorry, Damon, but ...'

'Are you going to tell me you don't want me to make love to you?'

'N—no, but ...'

'I'm glad you have at least that much honesty,' his voice shook with anger, 'you didn't exactly give me the impression you were a disinterested bystander.'

'I ... I'm sorry, Damon, I got carried away ...'

'*Carried away?*' His contempt seared her.

'Ye—yes. I suppose I had a little too much wine, and ...'

'There's a very vulgar name for girls like you, Philippa,' he snapped, his face a mask of fury.

'Please, Damon! Please understand ... without love I ...'

'*Love*!' he hissed, his lips drawn back in a snarl of hate, 'love isn't in our *contract*, Philippa. That precious contract you're so keen on. You're getting plenty, don't expect love as well.' He leaned forward as if to strike her. Instinctively she shrank away from him.

'You disgust me,' he went on cruelly. 'I have more respect for the commonest slut than I have for girls like you!' He took a stride to the door and flung it open. 'I congratulate you on one thing,' he rasped, 'you've successfully killed any desire I felt for you. I wouldn't touch you now. I could stay all night and your precious virtue would be quite safe. But don't worry, I'm going—I won't inflict my presence on you any longer!'

He slammed the door and left her. Philippa heard him go downstairs, the back door opened and closed. She heard the crunch of shingle as he walked rapidly down the beach. Then there was silence and she was alone with only the sound of the surf, which seemed to mock her through the night.

# CHAPTER TEN

AFTER Damon had left her Philippa flung herself face down on the bed and wept as she had never wept before. If only she hadn't climbed up to see that stupid ruin! They would have been home now, with an unsullied memory of a perfect day for her to treasure. Or if she had given in to him, answered the call of her blood and surrendered, as she had longed to do so often. But no! In spite of her grief she knew she had been right to refuse him. Her unhappiness was bitter now, but she knew it would have been a hundred times worse to have woken up in the morning, lying beside him, and to have sensed, however faintly, his disdain, his sense of triumph.

When her storm of weeping subsided she limped to the window and looked down the moonlit beach. At the far end Damon was standing looking morosely out to sea. Her heart ached for him, but it was impossible for her to explain to him. He scared her now. His anger still felt like a whiplash, and she doubted if she could ever forget it.

Towards dawn she slept fitfully, lying fully clothed on the bed. When she woke to the early sun and the household sounds of the taverna she was filled with such a feeling of despair, it was like a palpable weight in her breast. She wondered how she would cope with her inevitable meeting with Damon, how he would treat her.

She found out soon enough. She had just finished splashing her face with cold water when he came to the bedroom. His face was grim, his beard showed black on his thin cheeks, and he looked years older than he had last night. He looked at her coldly, as if she were a stranger.

'The boat's due in fifteen minutes. I'll carry you if you're ready.'

'I can manage on my own, Damon.' Philippa had to control her voice to stop it trembling.

'As you wish.'

He left her and she hobbled painfully downstairs. She was unable to swallow the bitter coffee provided, and Damon also left his untasted.

When the boat arrived he gave her his arm, but he never looked at her, nor did he offer to carry her again. She was installed in the cabin of the tub that was to take them to the mainland, while he went on deck and ignored her for the trip.

At their destination he again gave her his arm, sat her in a café, and went to phone the villa for the chauffeur to bring the car, then he disappeared until the Daimler arrived. This time it was the chauffeur who helped Philippa to the car. Damon stood aloof. He drove them, with the chauffeur sitting in the front beside him, Philippa miserable in the back. He drove round vicious corkscrew curves at breakneck speed, and she wondered if they would make it in one piece, but she was so unhappy that she didn't really care.

They arrived at the villa with a squealing of brakes and Damon, cold as ice, helped her from the car into the house.

'Tusker! At last you're back. I thought you'd never get here!'

In the hall stood Martha, wearing brief hot-pink shorts and top, petite and immaculate, her pebbly brown eyes round with surprise.

After Philippa had recovered from her initial shock she glanced hastily at Damon, dreading his reaction to this unexpected visitor. But his face was impassive, she had no idea what he was thinking.

'Martha! What . . . what are you doing here?' she asked.

'That's not much of a welcome, Tusker. Aren't you glad to see me?' pouted her sister.

Philippa tottered to one of the hall chairs and collapsed into it. 'Of course I'm pleased to see you, Martha,' she said dishonestly, 'but it's . . . it's such a surprise. Why didn't you let me know you were coming?'

'It was all very sudden. I only managed to wangle a last-minute flight through the office. Things are slack right now. I thought a holiday was just what I needed . . . and here I am!'

Martha looked up at Damon who remained silent. 'To be honest with you, Damon,' she said, 'I wanted to apologise. I wasn't very nice to you in the past. I wanted to say . . . sorry.'

Philippa was dumbfounded; this was the first time she had ever heard her sister apologise to anyone. 'Why didn't you write a letter?' she blurted undiplomatically.

Never taking her eyes off Damon, Martha replied, 'Letters are such impersonal things. And you know what a lousy letter-writer I am.' She looked humbly at her brother-in-law. 'Am I forgiven, Damon? I'm truly sorry.'

'Don't grovel, Martha, there's no need,' he said, 'as a matter of fact it's fortunate that you're here. I have to leave for Herakleion immediately, and Philippa's hurt herself. You can look after her.'

'Of course,' Martha agreed unenthusiastically.

'Then I'll change and go,' said Damon. 'Will you be here this weekend, Martha?'

'If I'm welcome,' Martha said meekly.

'I'll see you then.' With a brief nod at Philippa he left the two sisters.

'He's such a bear, your husband,' Martha said

silkily, 'but I'm sure his bark is worse than his bite.'
She seemed to notice her older sister for the first time.
'What *have* you been up to, Tusker? You look a mess!'

Philippa looked down at herself. Her jeans were
torn and stained, her shirt was grubby, and her foot
was bandaged with a dirty piece of rag; moreover, her
eyes were still puffy from her crying jag, and ringed
with shadows of fatigue.

'I fell down a mountain,' she said.

'What a silly thing to do!' Martha was not noted for
sympathy.

Philippa's maid came at this moment, and with
genuine concern helped her mistress to her bedroom,
ran a bath for her, and removed the soiled bandage
from Philippa's swollen ankle. Later a doctor arrived,
summoned by Damon, she discovered. He declared
the sprain a slight one and ordered her to rest for a
few days. She got some comfort from the fact that
Damon had cared enough to call a doctor. But he
hadn't stayed around to find out the verdict. Her maid
informed her that the *kyrios* had driven away as soon
as he had showered and shaved.

Philippa dozed in her bed for the rest of the day,
utterly exhausted. At teatime Athena burst into her
bedroom with a tray of tea things. She had been out
with her friends when Damon and Philippa returned,
and had only just found out about the accident. She
was all loving sympathy, and Philippa had to blink
away tears of weakness at this demonstration of
affection. After Damon's coldness and Martha's lack
of interest this attention was overwhelming.

Philippa sipped the tea gratefully. 'You've met my
sister?' she asked Athena. A guarded look came over
the girl's face.

'Oh yes. I went with the car to meet her at the
airport last night.' She stirred her tea thoughtfully.
'She is not at all like you, Pippa.'

'No. I'm a lot taller,' Philippa agreed.

'I did not mean your appearance,' Athena said solemnly, 'although it is true she is not as beautiful.'

Startled, Philippa said, 'But she's the pretty one—everyone says so.'

'She is pretty. But she is not as . . . easy to like . . . as you are,' the girl said stubbornly.

It was clear that Martha and Athena had not hit it off too well, and Philippa diplomatically changed the subject.

Athena asked for details of the accident. She listened gravely to Philippa's lighthearted account, then she impulsively hugged her in her thin arms. When she broke away her eyes were wet with tears.

'Athena! Darling, what's wrong?' Philippa asked. 'Why are you crying?'

'I do not want to lose you, Pippa,' was the tearful reply, 'the way I lost my mother and my grandparents. Uncle Damon and I, we have been lonely for so long . . . I could not bear to lose you now.'

'Darling!' Philippa held her close again. 'It's only a little sprain.'

Athena smiled wanly. 'I know. But be more *careful*, Pippa.' She picked up the tray and prepared to leave. Then she turned and said, 'I love you very much, Pippa,' then bolted out of the room.

When Athena had left her Philippa lay back on the pillows. Unwittingly Athena had added to her distress. She had not realised how much Athena needed her, and the knowledge that the divorce would be yet another trauma for the child pained Philippa deeply.

Her ankle was not hurting now, but the pain in her heart didn't abate. What with Damon's coldness, and now the added guilt about Athena, she wasn't sure how well she was going to cope for the rest of her time in Crete.

Damon did not come near the villa until the day o

the reception. By then Philippa's ankle was practically healed, and she was walking around again almost as good as new—physically, that was. Emotionally she was still bruised and desperately unhappy. But she disciplined herself to behave normally before others. In any case Martha was so self-absorbed, and Athena so taken up with her friends, that if Philippa seemed more subdued than usual they did not notice.

She dressed for the party with special care, choosing a gown of chalk white crêpe that was cut on the bias. It was extremely simple, and only when she moved did one notice that the dress clung to every sensuous curve of her slender body. The bodice was knotted over her breast, leaving her tanned shoulders bare. She searched through the jewel box Damon had given her in Athens, and found a necklace of diamonds, single stones strung at regular intervals on a thin platinum chain. She piled her wealth of pale hair on top of her head and twisted the diamonds through it. Her only other jewellery was a pair of diamond ear-rings. She was so brown that apart from her eyes she no longer needed make-up. A touch of natural lip-gloss, and she was ready.

Steeling herself for her first meeting with Damon since their return from Roumeli, she went out on the terrace to check on the last-minute arrangements. He was already there with Martha and Athena. He looked drawn and tired, even the superbly tailored white dinner jacket he wore failed to give him his usual debonair appearance.

'Pippa, you look lovely!' Athena said involuntarily. 'Doesn't she, Uncle Damon?'

For the first time since their quarrel he looked at her directly. Her heart contracted with pity. She had never seen such sadness on his face before. But the sadness was momentary, and was quickly replaced with a bitter expression. His mouth grew hard.

'Very appropriate.' He sounded bitter.

Athena prattled on innocently, 'Appropriate? How do you mean?'

'In that dress, and with the diamonds, she looks like snow and ice,' he said, and then added in a low voice, 'the correct dress for an ice maiden.'

It was clear he had not forgiven her, and Philippa summoned up her courage for the night ahead.

'Damon, your house is absolutely gorgeous!' Martha gushed, 'I'm simply overwhelmed. Did you design it yourself?' She gazed up at him adoringly.

'My father drew up the original plans,' Damon replied. 'He built the villa as a wedding gift for my mother.'

'How romantic!' Martha cooed. She turned to her sister. 'You are a lucky girl, Tusker,' she said, 'to have married into such a dashing family,' she turned back to her brother-in-law, 'and such a handsome one.'

His brows rose ironically. 'I'm delighted you approve, Martha,' he said. He turned away from her, but she caught his sleeve with her little claw-like hand, so that he was forced to look down at her again.

'I'm so glad we're friends, Damon,' she whispered. She turned to Philippa. 'You treat him properly, you hear Tusker?' she said. 'He's a real catch!'

Athena stifled an exclamation of disgust and said. 'Please excuse me. I will join you presently.' She glared at Martha and hurried from the room, clearly not trusting herself to remain in the other girl's presence another minute. Detaching himself from Martha's grasp, Damon also left them. Philippa turned on her little sister.

'Martha, for heaven's sake stop paying Damon such extravagent compliments! You embarrass him.'

Martha opened her eyes wide, a look of innocence on her face. 'I'm just being nice to him, Tusker That's what you want, isn't it?'

'You don't have to go to such extremes,' Philippa said. 'It's one thing to be polite, but you don't have to act like some sort of groupie.'

Martha looked wounded. 'Why, Phil, I do believe you're jealous!'

'I'm nothing of the kind. I just don't enjoy seeing you make a fool of yourself,' Philippa explained.

'You really mustn't be so possessive, Tusker,' Martha scolded sweetly, 'you'll never keep a man that way.' She smoothed the skirt of her electric blue dress. 'Even though you're older than me, Phil, you've not had much experience with men. Damon's such a man of the world. The last thing he wants is a clinging wife.'

Fortunately the first guests arrived at that moment, preventing Philippa from making a heated reply.

The party was a great success, but it was an ordeal for Philippa. Damon contrived to appear quite normal towards her in front of their guests, while subtly letting her know he was still furious. Martha was never far from his side, and Philippa found herself getting more and more irritated by her.

After the cocktail party they went to the hotel for the official reception and dance, where she and Damon had the honour of being the first couple on the new dance floor. In spite of the warmth of the evening Philippa felt a shiver run through her when he put his arm round her. He held her with great formality, as if she were a stranger, his eyes focused somewhere above her head. As soon as other couples joined them he bowed to her with chilling politeness, and after escorting her back to their table excused himself and disappeared.

That was the only dance they had together the whole night. Philippa danced with other guests, and saw Damon on the floor many times, always with a different partner. Once Martha grabbed him and insisted he dance a samba with her. When it ended he gave her one of his brief bows and left her standing alone on the floor.

Philippa rose early the next morning to discover that Athena had already left to spend the next few days with her friends. She had a shrewd suspicion the girl wanted to get away from Martha for a while.

Damon was already at the dining patio. He was seated on the balustrade, swinging his long legs, his cup of coffee on the stone ledge beside him. He looked round briefly when Philippa joined him and nodded tersely. She was about to make an attempt to talk to him when Martha joined them, and all hope of intimate conversation was destroyed. Martha chattered on about the party, and the elegance of the hotel, and how clever Damon was to head such an operation. She seemed oblivious of the atmosphere of stony silence hanging over Damon like a cloud.

Suddenly Philippa felt that if she didn't get away from the villa, from Damon's black mood, and Martha's inane chatter, she'd go mad. She put aside her coffee cup and announced that she was leaving on a small excursion to visit the remains of the post-Minoan city of Phalasarna a few kilometres to the west. Courtesy made her invite Martha, but knowing her sister's lack of interest in history she was pretty sure she would get a refusal.

Martha gave Damon's back a speculative look. 'Are you going to visit these mouldy old ruins, Damon?' she asked.

'I have work to do here,' Damon replied, still looking out to sea.

'Then I'll stay here too, and keep you company,' Martha said.

Damon turned round then, and ignoring Martha said to Philippa, 'I'll be leaving for Herakleion tonight, Philippa. That will be my base for the remainder of the summer. You'll have the villa pretty much to yourself from now on.'

She understood him. He was making it quite plain that he no longer enjoyed her company. She nodded curtly, and after some desultory conversation with Martha made her escape.

She drove west along the coast road, but even the wild geraniums splashing their colour on the hillside failed to relieve her depression. She stopped at a beach she had often visited before, and after exchanging a few pleasantries with one of the fishermen who was mending his nets on the sands, she swam vigorously for about half an hour. Then she lay in the buoyant water and tried to feel relief that soon she would be on her own. She could stay in Chania with Athena, and hardly ever have to see Damon again. It would help explain their break-up to the girl, and lessen the shock when she found out that her new aunt had returned to England for good in the autumn. Damon's departure was really a very good thing, Philippa kept telling herself. But no matter how hard she tried to convince herself the sadder she became.

Irritated, she pulled on her shorts and decided on the spur of the moment to return to the villa instead of visiting Phalasarna. She was a great believer in action rather than brooding when in the depths of depression, and cooking was the best action she knew. She would go straight to the kitchen and cook something difficult. It would take her mind off her troubles for a time. The thought of doing something positive, no matter how mundane, gave her energy and she drove back at full speed.

When she drove into the front driveway it was siesta hour and the villa was silent. The kitchen was deserted. Philippa found an apron behind the pantry door and started assembling the necessary ingredients for *filo* dough. That should keep her occupied for an hour, she decided. She had just taken the crock of butter from the fridge when the door burst open and Martha, distraught and tearful, came running into the kitchen. Philippa put down the crock and stared at her wild-eyed sister.

'Tusker! Oh, thank goodness you've come home!' Martha sobbed, 'I've been so frightened!'

Philippa put her arm round the trembling girl. 'Martha, what is it? Calm down, darling . . . what's the matter? Are you ill?' She led Martha to one of the kitchen chairs and gently sat her down.

'Oh, Tusker, it was so awful . . . I didn't know what to do . . .' Martha wailed incoherently. She buried her face in her hands and started to cry again.

Philippa filled a glass with water and handed it to Martha. 'Drink this, Martha . . . now tell me what's happened, darling. I can't help you till I know what's wrong.'

'I don't know how to tell you,' Martha moaned, 'it's so awful . . .' and she cried with renewed force.

Philippa spoke firmly. 'Now, Martha, stop it! Try and control yourself. You *must* tell me what's wrong.'

'It's . . . it's Damon . . .' the girl faltered.

Philippa went chalk white. Dread clutched at her. 'What do you mean? What about Damon? Has he had an accident?'

'Not him. He's fine,' Martha said bitterly, 'but he . . . he tried . . .'

'He tried *what*? Martha, for heaven's sake . . .' Philippa was feeling desperate now.

'He tried to rape me, that's what!' Martha declared. Philippa stared at her in disbelief.

'He did *what*?'

'He attacked me,' Martha replied. 'Look, he tore my dress.' She indicated the torn strap of her yellow sundress.

Philippa stared at her. 'I don't believe it,' she said.

'It's *true*,' Martha said sullenly. 'He came into my room at siesta time and tried to make love to me. When I pushed him away he tried to force me. Look! he bruised my arm.' She held out her left arm which showed a red mark above the elbow. 'Then he tried to tear my dress off. God knows what would have happened if we hadn't heard your car at that moment. He's an *animal*, Tusker!'

Philippa sank slowly into one of the chairs. She couldn't believe such an accusation. But a nightmare of doubt was stirring at the corner of her mind. Could she have been taken in by Damon all along? Love was blind, people said. Had she been blind? Was he the type of man who, having been refused by one sister, would try to force himself on the other? She shook her head. That didn't make sense. He didn't even *like* Martha. Surely he wouldn't force himself on a girl he despised. He could do better than that.

'I can see you don't believe me,' Martha said, 'but I tell you it's the *truth*! Maybe it's the custom in Crete for a man to sleep with his sister-in-law.' She clutched Philippa's arm painfully. 'I hate it here, Tusker, it's such a primitive place. Let's go home . . . to England. Please, Phil, take me home right now,' she begged. 'I can't bear it here another moment!'

'I can't leave just like that, Martha.' Philippa forced herself to be patient. 'There's Athena to think of. Besides, I must have this out with Damon.'

Martha looked horrified. 'No!' she exclaimed. 'Please, Phil—he's violent! Please come with me to the airport *now*, and let's go home.' She raised her voice another decibel. 'You don't seem to *understand*,' she wailed, 'I'm afraid to stay here! I'm afraid of what Damon might do to me . . . to you. He's *violent*, I tell you!' her voice soared out of control. 'Don't you realise what he tried to do? Don't you *care*? Take me home . . . I want to go home!'

'Pull yourself together, Martha!' Philippa ordered sharply. 'No one's going to hurt you. I can't go until I've talked to Damon.'

'What do you want to talk to him for?'

Philippa raised her voice to top Martha's anguished wail. 'I have to get his side of the story, Martha, that's only fair . . .'

'*Fair?* He wasn't fair with me! Don't you care about me at all, Tusker?'

'Don't be silly, Martha. Of course I care about you. But I care about Damon too . . .' Her voice broke, then she recovered herself. 'This has been a shock for me. You're accusing . . . someone I love,' again the tears came into her voice, 'someone I love very much. I *have* to talk to him, get his version.'

'My version of what?'

Martha jumped up with a smothered scream. Damon was standing at the open kitchen door. He was pale beneath his tan, and his pallor was accentuated by the black, coarse-textured linen shirt he was wearing.

'My version of what, Pippa?' he repeated, coming into the room and closing the door behind him.

'Don't listen to him, Tusker!' Martha shrieked. 'He'll deny everything. Please don't listen to him!'

Philippa waited for silence, then she quietly told Damon about Martha's accusation.

'Do you believe her, Pippa?' he asked when she had finished. 'Do you think I tried to force myself on your sister?'

She looked into his dark blue eyes. His level gaze never faltered. 'No, I don't believe her.' She turned to the frantic girl who crouched whimpering in the corner. 'Please, Martha, stop crying—you're not making things any better by crying.'

'Do you want to hear what really happened?' Damon asked.

'Don't listen to him, Tusker,' Martha wept, 'he's a liar, I tell you!'

Philippa put her arms around her sister. 'Hush, Martha!' she said. 'We must have the truth. Don't cry.' She kept Martha in her arms and turned to Damon. 'Tell me, Damon.'

'After lunch I went to my study to continue working. Martha went for a siesta,' he said. 'About ten minutes later she knocked at my door to ask if I could open her window, because it was stuck. I thought it odd that she didn't ask one of the servants, but I went to her room as she asked.' He stopped and looked at the two women. 'There was nothing wrong with her window,' he said, searching for words. 'When I tried to leave she stopped me, and . . . and offered herself to me.' Martha gave an ugly sob and tore herself out of Philippa's arms. 'She became hysterical when I refused her,' he went on. 'Then we heard your car arrive. I left her . . . and the rest you know.'

'You tore my dress!' Martha hissed. 'And my arm's bruised!'

'You did that to yourself, Martha,' Damon said coldly, 'to incriminate me. I didn't touch you.'

Totally bewildered, Philippa looked at her sister. 'Why, Martha?' she asked. 'Why did you do such a thing . . . tell such a wicked lie? I don't understand.'

Like a wild animal Martha bared her teeth in an ugly snarl and said savagely. 'I wanted to get back at you, Tusker, to make you pay for what you'd done!'

'What had I done?' Philippa quavered. 'How have I hurt you, Martha?'

'You had no right to get married before me . . . and to such a catch. *I'm* the pretty one, not you!' Her mouth turned down. 'It's not fair!' she seethed.

Philippa's lovely eyes filled with tears. 'Oh, Martha! I had no idea you hated me so much . . .' she said brokenly. She shook her head blindly.

'I planned it all in London,' Martha went on. Now she had started her confession she seemed unable to stop. 'I planned to come here and break up your marriage, take Damon away from you. If he'd wanted I would marry him. If not, I'd get you to leave him and come back with me. Either way, I would have won.'

'*Marry Damon?*' Philippa looked at her sister in astonishment. 'Do you love Damon, Martha?'

'Love him? I hate him! I always have. I'm not like you,' Martha sneered, 'taken in by the first man that makes a pass at you.'

'I think it's time you left us alone, Martha,' said Damon, his face sombre.

'Don't worry, I'm going!' Martha snapped. 'I won't stay in this house a minute more than I have to!' She turned at the door and looked at them both venomously. 'You've won this time. But I'll get even—just you wait and see!'

After Martha had left them Philippa let out a shuddering sigh. Martha's revelation had left her drained. She turned to Damon.

'I don't know what to say, Damon. I'm terribly sorry for . . . for everything. I had no idea she was so . . . full of hate. I . . . I . . .' She couldn't continue.

'She's not responsible, Pippa,' he said. 'Tell me, has Martha ever had any kind of . . . of emotional trouble?'

'She had a breakdown when our mother died,' Philippa admitted reluctantly.

'And now she thinks she's lost you too,' he said quietly. 'Poor Martha! I'm no psychiatrist, Pippa, but it seemed apparent from my first meeting with her that she was emotionally disturbed. Her extreme jealousy of you—it wasn't rational. She's always punished you for being all the things she's not.'

Philippa gave a strangled sob. 'Don't, Damon! I didn't realise . . .'

'I think we can help her, Pippa.' His compassion threatened to break her flimsy control. 'I know a first-rate therapist back in London. When she's calmer we'll persuade her to see him. She's young, she can be helped, I'm sure. Given time . . .'

Philippa interrupted, 'That's kind of you, but I can't ask you to put yourself out for Martha . . . nor for me. I think perhaps it would be better if I left too. I don't think it's right for me to stay under your roof any more. Perhaps Athena can stay with her friends for the rest of the summer. I'll leave with Martha and . . .' She didn't trust herself to say any more.

'Oh no, you don't, Pippa,' he said gently. 'Not so fast! He stood, barring her way. 'I'm not in the habit of listening at doors, but I couldn't help overhearing you and Martha.' He put his hand under her chin, tilting her face up, gazing deep into her troubled amber eyes. 'You said you loved me, Pippa. Is it true?' Her long lashes drooped and the blood slowly rose to her cheeks. 'The truth, now, Pippa. Do you love me?'

'Yes . . . yes,' she breathed, 'I'm afraid I do.'

'Afraid?' He let her go.

'I know you don't want that, Damon,' she explained, 'it wasn't part of our agreement.'

'Oh, Pippa . . . Pippa darling! Is that what you think?'

'No emotional entanglements,' she said, 'you spelled it out, chapter and verse.'

'God, I'm such a fool!' Damon muttered vehemently. 'I said that because I thought it was what *you* wanted. I've been emotionally entangled since I first laid eyes on you.'

'Wh-what?'

'Way back in April . . . in England . . . I kept having dinner parties, giving the servants the day off so you would come and cook for me. They've never had so many holidays!'

'Why didn't you say anything then?' Philippa could feel joy stirring in her like a fountain.

'Because you didn't like me at all. If I'd told you how I felt you'd never have come back.' He took hold of her unresisting hand. 'You didn't like me at first, did you, Pippa? Be honest.'

'Well, not at first. But I grew to like you quite soon.' She smiled up at him.

He turned away from her and gave a snort of disbelief. 'I'm a complete *fool*, my darling!' he told her. 'The *time* I've wasted! I devised this whole scheme because I wanted to get you all to myself. I hoped you'd learn to love me in time ... you know ... "Seeds Of April".' She looked at him uncomprehendingly. 'The poem by Browning I quoted to you once ... "You'll love me yet! ... From seeds of April's sowing."'

'Then that story about needing a wife, as a chaperone for Athena,' Philippa said, 'wasn't that true?'

'Oh yes, that was true. But the business arrangement part, that was my own plan. I thought if I didn't scare you away by telling you how much I loved you, you'd learn to care for me in time. Sometimes I thought I was beginning to succeed, but then you'd draw away from me and become cold again.'

'I didn't want to give myself away,' she admitted.

'In Athens I had hope.' He smiled, 'You seemed jealous of Thalia.'

'I was jealous,' she confessed. 'You spent the whole evening talking to her.'

'Talking about you. Telling her how in love I was,' he explained. 'Poor Thalia, I think she was thoroughly bored!' He cupped her face in his strong hands. 'I'm not dreaming, my dearest darling? You do love me?'

'I love you,' she said huskily. 'I'll never love anyone else.'

He kissed her then, folding his arms around her, holding her as if he would never let her go. When the kiss ended he still cradled her in his arms. 'Why did you reject me in Roumeli, Pippa?' he whispered.

'Oh, Damon!' she clung close to him. 'Because I thought you didn't love me. I couldn't give myself to you without love—it would have hurt too much. And then you were so angry...' She shivered at the memory.

He groaned with pain. 'My darling, can you ever forgive me? I wanted you so desperately. For weeks I'd longed to take you in my arms, possess you. When you pushed me away, I thought you meant that you could *never* love me, that you found me unattractive. I was in despair... in torment... and so I lashed out at you.' His eyes were almost black with misery. 'I have a terrible temper, Pippa, and when I lose control...'

She traced the line of his jaw with her finger and felt him tremble at her touch. 'It doesn't matter now, darling. As long as you love me nothing else matters.' She kissed his cheek and felt his breath quicken. 'If only you'd told me you loved me that night in Roumeli!'

'I was afraid of scaring you away.'

She gave a smothered cry, half laugh, half sob, and burrowed her head into his shoulder. Damon kissed the silky mass of hair on top of her head.

'When I finish my work here,' he said, 'we'll go on our honeymoon. Let's take the yacht and sail through the islands. Would you like that? And we'll make up for all the time we've wasted, eh?' He gently rained a trail of kisses down her cheek until his lips rested in the hollow of her throat.

Philippa sighed with pleasure. 'And after the honeymoon, darling, where do we go?'

'Home to England, to our house in Wimbledon.' He hugged her close and there was laughter in his voice.

'My darling, you only know the kitchen and dining room of your new home. I hope you'll like the rest of it?'

'I'll love it,' she assured him, but he was suddenly serious.

'What about your work, Pippa? Won't you miss it? Miss being independent? Miss the challenge of running your own business?'

She eased herself out of his embrace and thought for a moment before replying. 'I don't know, Damon,' she said. 'Right now I'm too full of happiness to answer you. But I do love my work. I find cooking so ... creative. I shall miss that.'

He reached for her hands and held them in his strong ones. 'I'd go into mourning if you never cooked again, my love!' he told her. 'Don't forget I'm your biggest fan. But if you're unhappy without your work we'll work something out, I promise. I'd never insist you give up something important to you, Pippa. Just remember that you have a challenging role to play in my life, dearest. I need you as my hostess, as my partner, and I want you for my companion. I want you to be free to travel with me. And when the children come ...'

'Ah yes—the children.' Philippa caught her breath with delight.

'Then we'll *both* travel less,' he promised.

Philippa was reminded of Athena back in Athens babbling happily about future 'brothers and sisters'.

'Damon,' she asked, 'if she wanted to, could Athena come and live with us in London?'

'Would you like that, Pippa? To have Athena with us?'

'Yes, I would,' she said. 'I've grown to love her dearly.'

His eyes glittered suspiciously. He lifted her hands to his lips and tenderly kissed them. 'My dearest love,' he murmured hoarsely, 'my dearest love.'

He enfolded her in his arms again, and they stood silently for a long while; then with one of his mercurial changes of mood he thrust her away and looked at his watch.

'Pippa! We've just got time,' he exclaimed.

'Time?' she queried.

'To catch the boat to Roumeli. Let's go back now, darling, let's wipe out that black memory for ever.'

She nodded happily. She would follow him to the ends of the earth if he asked her.

Late that night Philippa lay beside her husband in the taverna in Roumeli. Moonlight flooded the white-washed room, illuminating the simple furnishings.

Damon leaned over her, stroking her honey-blonde hair which streamed over the pillow.

'My lovely, passionate wife,' he murmured, kissing the tender hollow beneath her collar bone.

'Damon,' she gave a throaty chuckle, 'when we get back . . . let's tear up the contract.'

He pulled her into his arms, and with a happy sigh she arched against him, responding to him joyfully, knowing the time for pretence was over, and she need never hide her love from him again.

## THE LEGEND OF ACHILLES' HEEL

At five-foot-ten, Philippa feels (however misguidedly) that she is too tall to be attractive, and she considers her height to be her "Achilles' heel." This interesting expression comes from the story of a warrior hero of ancient Greece.

Achilles was born the son of Thetis, a water nymph, and Peleus, the king of Thessaly. Though Thetis was immortal, her son was not. To make her infant's body invincible, she held him by the heel and dipped him into the sacred waters of the River Styx.

When Achilles was nine, the Greeks declared war on Troy. The prophet Calchas predicted that only Achilles could conquer that city. Thetis, however, had been warned that her son would die there. She disguised Achilles as a girl and hid him among the many daughters of King Lycomedes of Skyros. One day Odysseus, the king of Ithaca, traveled to Lycomedes' palace. He presented the king's daughters with gifts of jewels—but suspecting the presence of Achilles, cleverly hid weapons among them. The girls took the jewels, and the disguised Achilles was discovered when he immediately reached for the weapons! Unable to avoid his destiny, Achilles was soon off to the Trojan War.

The handsome young Greek became a brave hero, slaying the great Trojan warrior Hector. But Paris, the son of King Priam of Troy, shot an arrow at him, which, guided by the god Apollo, struck Achilles in the very heel that the waters of the Styx had not touched—and therefore not made invincible. Achilles soon died from his wound.

That is why, when we have a weakness among all our strengths, it is called an "Achilles' heel."

# HARLEQUIN CLASSIC LIBRARY

Great old romance classics from our
early publishing lists.

**FREE BONUS BOOK**

On the following page is a coupon with
which you may order any or all of these titles.
If you order all nine, you will receive a FREE
book—*District Nurse*, a heartwarming classic
romance by Lucy Agnes Hancock.

The fourteenth set
of nine novels in the

**HARLEQUIN CLASSIC LIBRARY**

# Great old favorites...
# Harlequin Classic Library

Complete and mail this coupon today!

**FREE BONUS BOOK**

## Harlequin Reader Service

In U.S.A.
1440 South Priest Drive
Tempe, AZ 85281

In Canada
649 Ontario Street
Stratford, Ontario N5A 6W2

Please send me the following novels from the Harlequin Classic Library. I am
enclosing my check or money order for $1.50 for each novel ordered, plus 75¢
to cover postage and handling. If I order all nine titles at one time, I will receive
a FREE book, *District Nurse*, by Lucy Agnes Hancock.

☐ 118  ☐ 121  ☐ 124
☐ 119  ☐ 122  ☐ 125
☐ 120  ☐ 123  ☐ 126

| | |
|---|---|
| Number of novels checked @ $1.50 each = | $_____ |
| N.Y. and Ariz. residents add appropriate sales tax | $_____ |
| Postage and handling | $_____.7 |
| TOTAL | $_____ |

I enclose _____
(Please send check or money order. We cannot be responsible for cash sent
through the mail.)
Prices subject to change without notice.

Name _____
    (Please Print)

Address _____
         (Apt. no.)

City _____

State/Prov. _____

Zip/Postal Code _____

Offer expires February 29, 1984     30856000X

## Choose from this list of handsome, hardbound Romance Treasury volumes — each a delightful collection of 3 great Harlequin Romances!

**Complete and mail coupon
on following page today!**

# Collect a love-story library with
## *Romance Treasury*

Complete and mail this coupon today!

**Harlequin Reader Service**

In the U.S.A.
1440 South Priest Drive
Tempe, AZ 85281

In Canada
649 Ontario Street,
Stratford, Ontario N5A 6W2

Please send me the following Romance Treasuries. I am enclosing
my check or money order for $6.97 for each Treasury ordered plu
75¢ to cover postage and handling.

      ☐ *Volume 9*        ☐ *Volume 63*

      ☐ *Volume 33*     ☐ *Volume 66*

      ☐ *Volume 44*     ☐ *Volume 69*

      ☐ *Volume 51*     ☐ *Volume 72*

      ☐ *Volume 60*     ☐ *Volume 76*

Number of Treasuries checked @ $6.97 each = $_____

N.Y. and Ariz. residents add appropriate sales
tax.                                   $_____

Postage and handling                $_____75

I enclose   TOTAL  $_____

(Please send check or money order. We cannot be responsible for cash sent throug
the mail.)
Prices subject to change without notice.

NAME_____

ADDRESS_____
                              (APT. NO.)

CITY_____

STATE/PROVINCE_____

ZIP/POSTAL CODE_____
Order while quantities last. **Offer expires February 29, 1984**    308560000

# What the press says about Harlequin romance fiction...

"When it comes to romantic novels...
Harlequin is the indisputable king."
— *New York Times*

"...exciting escapism, easy reading, interesting
characters and, always, a happy ending....
They are hard to put down."
— *Transcript-Telegram*, Holyoke (Mass.)

"...always...an upbeat, happy ending."
— *San Francisco Chronicle*

"...a work of art."
— *Globe & Mail*, Toronto

"Nothing quite like it has happened since
*Gone With the Wind...*"
— *Los Angeles Times*